Boogeyman

Andrew C. Howard

Published by NoNy Mouse House Publishing, 2024.

BOOGEYMAN

First edition. October 29, 2024.

Copyright © 2024 Andrew C. Howard.

ISBN: 979-8227380173

Written by Andrew C. Howard.

Table of Contents

This book is dedicated to the women and children who are victims of assault.

Special Thanks:

Anfal Ahmed & Paul Lappen

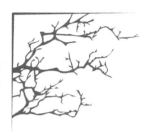

Chapter One

"You take the blue pill, the story ends, you wake up in your bed and believe whatever you want to believe. You take the red pill, you stay in wonderland, and I show you how deep the rabbit hole goes." – Morpheus, *The Matrix*

In the heart of Thornfield, where time seemed to sway with the rustling leaves and secrets whispered among ancient trees, a tale unfolded—one that wove the threads of reality and nightmare into an intricate tapestry. Thornfield, with its serene charm masking deeper mysteries, held within its embrace the essence of a world where young Amelia would soon find herself entangled in a dance between light and shadow, truth and illusion.

With her golden locks cascading like sunlight upon her slender shoulders, Amelia was the epitome of innocence. Her laughter, like tinkling bells, echoed through the neighborhood, bringing joy to even the sternest of faces. Her blue eyes sparkled with a light that could chase away the darkest clouds, and her presence was a ray of sunshine in the lives of those who knew her. But beneath her infectious smile, a darkness lay dormant, waiting patiently to emerge.

On one fateful night, when the moon hung like a pale, battered lantern in the inky sky, young Amelia drifted into a seemingly serene slumber. Innocence, however, proved to be no armor against the encroaching malevolence lurking within her very own sanctuary.

It began subtly, as horrors often do, seeping into the nooks and crannies of her dreamscape. The first sign was a whisper, so faint it could have been mistaken for the wind rustling through the leaves outside her window. But this whisper carried with it a chill that made the hair on the back of her neck stand on end. As the night deepened, the whispers grew louder, slithering forth from the murky depths, weaving nightmares into the fabric of her mind. Shadows danced wickedly across the walls, elongating and distorting until they became grotesque monstrosities, morphing into the embodiment of her deepest fears.

And there, within the confines of her closet, the timeless terror that generations had feared stirred with a hunger for chaos. The Boogeyman emerged from the obscurity of the relentless night, his twisted visage basked in the dim glow of a half-forgotten nightlight. His form was a dark, amorphous mass, eyes glowing with a malevolent intelligence that seemed to pierce through the very fabric of Amelia's soul. Somewhere deep within the twisted corridors of her fractured mind, Amelia's innocence was held captive, shackled by the chains of her own fear.

In these darkest hours, when silence blanketed the town and the moon whispered secrets that only the shadows could decipher, the real Amelia emerged—a girl possessed by terror, captivated by an unseen terror that clawed and gnawed at the edges of her sanity. Each passing hour intensified the malignant force within her, feeding it fears and anxieties until it swelled with a malevolence unprecedented in the hallowed tales of Thornfield's past.

For Amelia, however, there was no turning back. With each passing hour, the Boogeyman claimed another fragment of her true self, shackling her to a macabre existence filled with tortured dreams and insomnia-drenched nights. The dreams became more vivid, the terror more real. She would wake, drenched in sweat, her heart pounding in her chest, but the images would remain, burned into her mind like a brand.

In the haunting realm where dreams bled into reality, Amelia's destiny hung precariously in the balance, her fragile existence teetering on the precipice of a terrifying unknown. The Boogeyman was no mere childhood phantasm, but a malevolent force that aimed to shroud the town in perpetual night.

As the curtains of twilight brushed against the trembling horizon of reality, we step into a world where innocence is devoured, and the only solace lies within the unrelenting resilience of the human spirit. For inside the tragic tale of Amelia, the true horrors await—horrors that could only be conjured within the realm of Freddy's nightmares.

Each night became a battle, not just for sleep, but for sanity. Her parents, though supportive, were helpless in the face of an enemy they couldn't see or understand. They watched, hearts breaking, as their vibrant daughter became a shadow of herself, haunted by fears they could neither comprehend nor dispel.

Yet, in the depths of her despair, there remained a glimmer of hope. Amelia, despite the horrors that plagued her, was a fighter. She clung to the fragments of light that broke through the darkness, finding strength in the smallest of things—a kind word from a friend, the warmth of the sun on her face, the fleeting moments of peace that came when she was awake. These small mercies were her lifeline, a reminder that there was still beauty in the world, still reasons to fight.

And so, the battle continued. The Boogeyman, relentless in his pursuit, faced a formidable opponent in the form of a young girl whose spirit refused to be broken. The nights were long and filled with terror, but with each dawn, Amelia found a renewed sense of determination. The darkness may have been vast, but it was not impenetrable, and Amelia was prepared to fight until her last breath to reclaim the light.

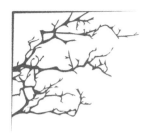

Chapter Two

NIGHT AFTER NIGHT, as the moon hung high in the yawning sky, Amelia found herself ensnared in a dance with terror. Her bed, once a sanctuary against the demons that lurked within the shadows, had morphed into a prison of the mind, a labyrinthine trap that held her captive in the clammy embrace of fear itself. The once-soft sheets felt like chains, binding her to a place where nightmares reigned supreme. Each night, the ritual began anew, with Amelia's heart pounding a frantic rhythm as she tucked herself under the covers, hoping against hope that this night might be different.

There, in the suffocating darkness, the Boogeyman – a phantom specter sculpted from the deepest recesses of childhood nightmares – prowled with an insidious stealth. Invisible to all but his chosen prey, his presence wrapped around Amelia like a vice, grinding into her very bones. She could feel him, even when she couldn't see him, a cold, malevolent force that pressed down on her chest, making it hard to breathe. The air itself seemed to thicken, suffused with the stench of decay and the acrid tang of fear.

In the midst of this unyielding grip, Amelia's voice rose in desperate crescendo, piercing the thick shroud of dread that consumed her. Like a wounded animal calling for solace, she would scream, her pleas echoing through the winding corridors of her childhood home, reaching the ears of her guardians – her protectors against the sinister unknown that swirled beneath her trembling eyelids. Her cries were heart-wrenching, a blend of pure terror and utter helplessness, the kind that tore at the soul and left deep, invisible scars.

Time and again, they would rush to her side, fueled by a blend of love and concern. But the beast Amelia dared to define as "Boogeyman" was a master of illusion, a cunning predator who vanished in the blink of an eye. As Amelia's parents burst into the room, armed with warmth and reassurances, the nightmare that plagued her would dissipate like a phantom mist – its presence evaporating without a trace. They would hold her, whispering soothing words, trying to chase away the lingering shadows with their love. Yet, each time they left, the room seemed darker, the air colder, the shadows deeper.

Yet, Amelia knew in the depths of her soul that she was not fabricating these nocturnal horrors, nor was she losing her grip on reality like a tethered balloon caught in an errant gust of wind. The Boogeyman, in all his diabolical malevolence, was real – as tangible as the goosebumps that trailed like braille across her skin. She could feel his eyes on her, could hear his breath, a rasping whisper that sent shivers down her spine. Each night, the fear grew, an insidious force that gnawed at her sanity, eroding her sense of safety and reality.

Each night, when the tranquility of slumber should reign supreme, Amelia remained vigilant, her heart pounding within the confines of her chest. The clock ticked away in fevered torment as she stared at the ceiling, imprisoned by the enigmatic specter that haunted her very existence. Sleep became an elusive dream, a distant memory. She lay there, her eyes wide open, every creak of the house, every rustle of the wind, a harbinger of impending doom. The Boogeyman, it seemed, had made her his prey – a cat and mouse game whose rules danced on the razor's edge of sanity. Amelia had become entwined in this twisted marathon, her fear and frustration veiled beneath a façade of seemingly mundane days.

And so, under the shadowy veil of moonlight, Amelia found herself caught in a web of terror spun with the ethereal threads of nightmarish dread. The battle against an unseen assailant raged on, her voice etched with desperation as she begged for sanctuary, for a reprieve from the ceaseless grip of fear's icy fingers. Yet, the nightmare persisted, the Boogeyman always one elusive step ahead, slipping away just as the world of the conscious encroached upon his realm. He was a phantom, an elusive shadow that could never be caught, always lurking just out of sight, a dark figure at the edge of her vision.

Amelia's fragile existence teetered on a precipice. Would she forever be trapped within the liminal space, forever caught in the clutches of a beast she could not see, nor intercept? The questions tormented her, the uncertainty gnawing at her peace of mind. Until the day dawned when the light of truth shone through the darkness, Amelia would remain suspended in a realm where reality and nightmare converged. Each dawn brought with it a faint glimmer of hope, a fragile thread that was quickly snapped by the weight of her terror.

And so, she braced herself for the unending nocturnal battles, where the invisible predator's shadow loomed over her, and the spectral dance between life and terror continued its macabre waltz. The nights stretched on, sleepless tendrils coiling around Amelia's weary mind like the skeletal fingers of a malevolent phantom. What once was a vibrant spirit, brimming with life and laughter, now hung like a tattered tapestry, its colors fading as the days slipped by. Her once bright eyes were now dim, shadowed by dark circles and the haunted look of someone who had seen too much.

Her parents, driven to the edge of desperation, sought aid from every doctor within reach, each visit tinged with the faint hope of unraveling the enigma that had ensnared their precious daughter. They went from one specialist to another, each promising answers but delivering none. The house was filled with the scent of herbal remedies, the hum of strange machines, and the quiet murmur of concerned conversations. But as time tangled itself into a cacophony of unanswered questions and mounting anxiety, the light of clarity seemed to flicker further away, a distant candle swallowed by the vast, consuming darkness.

Amelia's once echoing laugher vanished, hollowed by the unmerciful grip of whatever force held her captive. Her laughter, once a constant presence, was now a rare and brittle sound, as fragile as glass. No elixir or remedy could breach the impenetrable fortress that encased her tormented soul. The Boogeyman, with his malevolent grin, had taken root in her mind, a dark presence that overshadowed every moment of her life.

As the days turned into weeks, and weeks into months, Amelia's world shrank to the confines of her room, the shadows her only companions. She withdrew from her friends, her words replaced by silence. Her parents watched helplessly as their bright, joyful daughter became a shadow of her former self, her spirit crushed under the weight of a terror they could not see, nor understand. The Boogeyman, it seemed, had not only stolen Amelia's nights, but her days as well, casting a pall of fear over her once vibrant life.

In the face of such relentless darkness, Amelia's spirit remained unbroken, though battered and bruised. She clung to the faint hope that one day, the nightmare would end, and she would be free from the Boogeyman's grasp. Until then, she fought on, each night a battle, each day a struggle. For even in the deepest, darkest night, there is a glimmer of dawn, a promise of light that cannot be extinguished. And so, Amelia braced herself for the unending fight, her heart a fortress of resilience against the unyielding terror that sought to consume her.

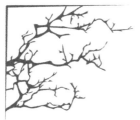

Chapter Three

THE HEART-WRENCHING decision loomed over her parents like an encroaching storm cloud, leaving its shadowy tendrils curled around their very hearts. To admit their beloved child to a sanitarium, a path fraught with uncertainty and pain, seemed to be the only refuge left amidst the tempest of despair. Perhaps there, within the cold, sterile walls, lay the sanctuary they so desperately sought. A sanctuary where solace intertwined with answers, a chance to finally unravel the twisted threads that had woven together her tortured existence.

As they whispered their tearful goodbyes, a sense of helplessness mingled with a morsel of fragile hope. They watched their precious daughter being ushered away, her small form swallowed by the depths of the sanitarium's yawning maw. The harsh fluorescents flickered with a sinister admonition, casting long, twisted shadows across the dreary corridor. In that moment, as the doors sealed shut behind her, the world seemed to shudder with uncertainty, as though unwittingly bearing witness to the unfolding horror that lay ahead.

Their plea for answers echoed through the cavernous halls, swept away by the frigid gusts of fate. The doctors, with their well-intentioned eyes masked by harbingers of doubt, scoured through years of medical wisdom in a desperate pursuit for respite. They prodded, poked, and probed, like blind surgeons stumbling through an operation without an understanding of the ailment they sought to heal.

Amelia, confined within the sterile walls of the sanitarium, found solace amidst the cacophony of beeping monitors and swirling phantoms of medical staff. A prisoner of her own mind, she clung to the flickering hope that resided within the comforting embrace of those walls. Night after night, the ever-watchful doctors observed her, their eyes penetrating her fractured thoughts like razor-sharp scalpels. They ordered tests, countless tests, probing the depths of her mysterious affliction. Their relentless pursuit of answers filled her nights with oddly soothing lullabies, lulling her into an uneasy slumber.

Time became a blur within those suffocating walls, where the artificial lighting blazed like the eyes of demons, casting eerie shadows across her weakened frame. Days turned into weeks. Weeks bled into months. Time became an elusive specter, dancing far beyond their outstretched grasp. In the depthless pit of despair, sleep had deserted her, like a treacherous lover fleeing from the nightmare that had become her existence.

Amelia, her tenuous grasp on reality slipping away like sand through fragile fingertips, languished within the sterile prison. Her once vibrant laughter reduced to hollow echoes, her spirit entwined with the ever-deepening shadows that crept across the sanitarium wards. The walls, once a promise of sanctuary, now felt like the cold embrace of a relentless captor, their sterility mocking the warmth and freedom she yearned for.

The mystery that haunted her tormented existence remained cloaked in riddles, hiding its malevolence within the depths of her tortured mind. It prowled like a stealthy predator, reveling in her torment, savoring the damage wrought upon her fragile being. Every corner of the sanitarium seemed to harbor whispers of her fear, each creak and groan of the building amplifying the terror that clung to her like a second skin.

Amidst the trials and tribulations, Amelia's parents clung to the flickering candle of hope, praying for a breakthrough they knew might never come. They stood on shifting sands, at the precipice of despair, teetering on the edge of a chasm that threatened to swallow them whole. Their visits, filled with forced smiles and desperate reassurances, were a fragile lifeline, a tenuous connection to the world outside the sanitarium's oppressive walls.

Yet, in the face of darkness, there still flickered a dim ember, a fragile light seeking refuge amidst the shadows. Their determination burned like a beacon, birthing a resolve that refused to crumble beneath the weight of the unknown. Each passing day, their hope became a battle cry, a defiant stand against the consuming darkness that sought to claim their daughter.

For, even in the darkest corners of existence, where nightmares festered like grotesque manifestations of the mind, the will to survive endured. And so, they clung to that hope, their fragile anchor in a sea of uncertainty, praying that one day, against all odds, it would guide them to the answers they desperately sought. Their faith, though tested, remained unbroken, a testament to the love and desperation that fueled their tireless quest for their daughter's salvation.

But gradually, in the whispers of Trazodone and tender touches as she performed the Thorazine shuffle, sleep began to rekindle the dying ember in her battered heart. Shadows morphed into distant memories, monsters dissipated into whispers of faded dreams. The doctors, their words dripping with honeyed promises, told her she was on the mend, that her torturous ordeal was reaching its long-awaited conclusion. They deemed her stable enough for release from the very jaws of the beast that had consumed her sanity.

The day of her liberation arrived like a cruel joke, the sun's rays piercing through her window like accusatory fingers. She stared at the expanse of blue sky outside, the color mocking her frailty, her desperate longing for normalcy. The doctors, with their false smiles and rehearsed platitudes, assured her that she was ready to reenter a world she could no longer recognize.

Amelia, straddling the precipice between salvation and damnation, clung to the doctor's promise like a drowning soul clings to driftwood. Stepping out of the sanitarium, the cool breeze brushing her face, she forced herself to believe that the darkness was behind her. But as the building's imposing façade loomed ever smaller in the rearview mirror, a pang of unease crept into her heart.

For in the realm of darkness, even the sweetest reprieve can hide a lurking horror, and the battle for one's sanity is never truly over. The shadows that once haunted her dreams seemed to whisper from the depths of her memory, a reminder that some battles, once begun, never truly end.

In the end, it was this combined force of love, determination, and unyielding hope that would light the path forward. Amelia's story was far from over, and within the walls of the sanitarium, a new chapter was waiting to be written—a chapter where light would finally triumph over darkness, and where the Boogeyman would be banished to the realm of forgotten nightmares.

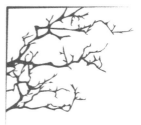

Chapter Four

RETURNING HOME SHOULD have been a joyous occasion, a welcomed embrace of the familiar, but for Amelia, it was a bittersweet reunion. The worn-out siding of the old house, a relic from the past, clung to her memories like moss on a decaying tombstone. Each creaking floorboard and chipped paint whispered tales of her childhood, but they also harbored the shadows of her recent torment. She tried her best to throw herself into the arms of normalcy, cherishing each mundane moment as if it were a shimmering gem in her palm. Yet, deep within her soul, an underlying sense of unease clawed at her, a malicious whisper that refused to dissipate.

Days bled into weeks, the dawns breaking with a feeble promise of serenity. The mornings were filled with the comforting routine of breakfast with her parents, the smell of coffee mingling with the scent of freshly cut grass drifting in through the open windows. But the nights, oh, the nights were a different breed altogether. When the sun took its final bow and the darkness bared its jagged teeth, Amelia found herself imprisoned within a labyrinth of her own fears. An abyss opened up inside her mind, and she dared not step too close, for fear that the darkness would swallow her whole.

The comfort of her childhood bed felt like a distant memory as the nights stretched into an endless ordeal. The moonlight streaming through the curtains cast eerie, shifting patterns on the walls, transforming her room into a canvas of phantoms. Sleep became a fleeting dream, always just out of reach. Her nights were spent in restless vigilance, listening to the house settle around her with each creak and groan amplified into the sinister movements of unseen monsters.

But then, one wretched night, it happened. The night came alive with a symphony of sound and shadows. Amelia, tucked under layers of blankets, tried to stave off sleep as if it were a venomous serpent. She knew it was coming, the returning terror that danced its cruel ballet within the confines of her mind. The air grew stagnant, as if the very atmosphere held its breath in anticipation.

A creak, so subtle, yet deafening in the silence, pierced through the veil of her thoughts. It was just the house, she reasoned. The ancient bones of the structure settling under the weight of time. That's all it was. She repeated these words like a mantra, hoping to fend off the invisible hands that threatened to suffocate her. But beneath the fragile façade of her rationality, a primal instinct screamed, a wolf howling at the encroaching darkness.

The sound came again, louder this time, closer. A shiver chased its icy fingers down Amelia's spine, her skin prickling with goosebumps. Slowly, she swung her legs out from under the blankets, the cold floor sending an electric shock through her veins. She hesitated, her feet poised above the ground, as if upon the precipice of an unseen abyss. With a reluctant resolve, she took her first hesitant steps towards the looming terror that awaited her.

The house groaned in protest as she tiptoed through the dimly lit hallway, her fingertips barely grazing the peeling wallpaper. The air hung heavy with the scent of decay and secrets long thought buried. Amelia's heart hammered within her chest, an echo punctuating the eeriness of the night. She dared not breathe, terrified that even the slightest sound would awaken the lurking beast that had plagued her for far too long.

And then she saw it, a faint glimmer of light piercing the darkness. The door to the attic, a forbidden place filled with forgotten relics and shattered dreams, stood ajar. The insidious pull of curiosity overtook her, dragging her through the threshold and into the abyss she had long tried to avoid. As the staircase creaked beneath her weight, Amelia couldn't help but wonder if she was descending into madness as she ascended the stairs.

The attic, shrouded in inky blackness, greeted her with the weight of a thousand lost souls. Cobwebs clung to her hair and clothes, entangling her in a suffocating embrace. She squinted through the gloom, desperately searching for a glimmer of truth amidst the shadows. And there, in the far corner, a figure stood, its presence radiating a malevolence that sent tremors through Amelia's fragile frame.

With quivering hands, she activated the flashlight she had clutched like a lifeline, its feeble beam tearing through the nightmarish haze. And there it was, the abomination that haunted her dreams. Its eyes, vacant and hungry, bore into her very essence, stripping away layers of sanity with each passing second. As screams threatened to claw their way up her throat, Amelia knew she had returned home not only to her past but to the dark depths of her own soul.

As the blood-curdling scream tore through the silence of the old house, Amelia felt her body turn to ice. The flashlight slipped from her trembling hands and clattered onto the wooden floor, casting flickering circles of light on the worn carpet. Standing there, trapped in the grip of sheer terror, she could only watch as the darkness in front of her seemed to materialize into the nightmarish figure of the Boogeyman.

Every fiber of her being urged her to run, to escape this living nightmare that had invaded her home. She stumbled backward, her heart thundering in her chest, desperately making her way towards the stairs that would lead her to safety. But the specter, so familiar, whispered her name with malicious delight, its voice a chilling echo in the empty house.

Amelia's breath hitched as her foot caught on an unnoticed box, sending her sprawling downward. With each bone-jarring tumble, she shrieked, as if her very voice was a lifeline in this abyss of fear. Finally, she came to a halt, a heap of battered limbs and shattered courage, at the foot of the stairs.

Through the haze of pain and confusion, reality slowly seeped back into her consciousness. Her tear-filled eyes focused on the figure before her, and she realized with a mixture of relief and overwhelming emotion that it was her mom. In that moment of clarity, she clung to her mother, wrapping her shaking arms around her with a fierceness born of sheer survival.

Amelia tried to sob out the words, to communicate the terror that had consumed her, to make her mother understand the Boogeyman's presence in their home. But as the words struggled to shape themselves into coherent sentences, a new sound echoed from the darkness above.

It wasn't the Boogeyman emerging from the shadows, but her father, descending cautiously from the attic steps. Startled and bewildered, he found himself face-to-face with his daughter, her tear-streaked face and trembling frame revealing a world of unspeakable horrors she had just witnessed.

In any other circumstance, this revelation would have been comical, a misunderstanding that could have evoked laughter and relief. But in this moment, with the lingering tendrils of fear still tightly wound around their hearts, no one found amusement in the situation. Especially not the frightened and bruised Amelia, who sought solace in the familiar safety of her parents' embrace.

As she clung to her mother, the comfort of that embrace began to thaw the icy grip of terror. Her father, too, joined them, enveloping his daughter in a cocoon of familial love and protection. They stood there, a trio bound by blood and fear, united against the darkness that sought to tear them apart.

For Amelia, this moment of unity felt like a fragile lifeline. The shadows that had once seemed insurmountable now felt a little less daunting with her parents by her side. The Boogeyman might still lurk in the recesses of her mind, but here, in the arms of her family, she found a flicker of hope, a spark of resilience that refused to be extinguished.

They spent the rest of the night huddled together in the living room, the soft glow of the fireplace casting comforting shadows on the walls. Her mother brewed a pot of chamomile tea, its warm, soothing aroma filling the room and calming Amelia's frayed nerves. Her father, ever the protector, kept a watchful eye on the windows and doors, ensuring no real or imagined threats could penetrate their sanctuary.

As the first light of dawn broke through the darkness, Amelia felt a semblance of peace settle over her. The night had been a brutal reminder of the demons she still battled, but it had also shown her the strength that lay within her family's love. They were her anchors, her lifeline in the stormy sea of her fears.

Over the next few days, they talked openly about her experiences, sharing their fears and hopes with one another. Her parents' unwavering support and understanding helped to ease the burden of her anxiety, allowing her to confront her nightmares with renewed determination. They devised a plan to seek additional help, finding a therapist who specialized in trauma and anxiety disorders, someone who could guide Amelia through the labyrinth of her mind and help her reclaim her life.

With each passing day, Amelia grew stronger, more resolute. She resumed her daily routines, finding solace in the familiar rhythms of life. The garden, once a neglected patch of overgrown weeds, became her sanctuary. She spent hours tending to the plants, finding peace in the simple act of nurturing life. The vibrant colors of blooming flowers and the earthy scent of soil grounded her, reminding her that there was beauty and growth even in the midst of turmoil.

Nights, though still challenging, became less of a battleground. Armed with coping strategies and the unwavering support of her family, Amelia faced her fears head-on. She kept a journal by her bedside, pouring her thoughts and nightmares onto its pages, transforming her fear into words she could control and understand.

The attic, once a place of dread, was slowly transformed into a space of healing. With her parents' help, Amelia sorted through the forgotten relics and dusty memories, reclaiming the attic as a studio for her art. She painted the walls a soothing shade of blue and filled the room with canvases and brushes, creating a sanctuary where she could express her emotions freely.

Through her art, Amelia found a voice for her pain, a way to confront the Boogeyman that had haunted her dreams. Her paintings, vivid and raw, depicted her journey through darkness and into light. Each stroke of the brush was an act of defiance, a declaration of her resilience and strength.

As the seasons changed and the leaves turned golden, Amelia looked back on her journey with a sense of pride and accomplishment. She had faced her darkest fears and emerged stronger, more resilient. The Boogeyman still lingered in the shadows, but he no longer held power over her. She had reclaimed her home, her life, and her soul.

Returning home had indeed been a bittersweet reunion, but it had also been a journey of healing and transformation. Amelia had found strength in the love of her family, courage in the face of her fears, and hope in the promise of a brighter future. She stood at the threshold of her old house, looking out at the world with newfound determination, ready to embrace whatever lay ahead.

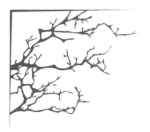

Chapter Five

THAT NIGHT, WITH EMOTIONS still raw and scars etched into her soul, Amelia cried herself to sleep in her parents' bed. The Boogeyman may have been banished, her father's presence offering a comforting reassurance, but the residue of fear continued to linger within the walls of their home. As the shadows danced on the edges of their nightmares, they knew that true security would forever be an illusion in the face of the unknown.

For what seemed like a lifetime, Amelia had been tormented by the Boogeyman, making its malevolent presence manifest in every corner of her life, squeezing tighter and tighter until she could hardly breathe. Sleep had become a treacherous dance with nightmares, the shadows becoming a playground for her deepest fears. Her parents watched helplessly as their beloved daughter slowly crumbled under the weight of this unseen terror, their attempts to comfort and protect her falling short.

Her father, a man of unwavering determination, refused to let despair consume him. He couldn't bear to see his precious girl suffer any longer. He had heard the whispers of the Boogeyman in the hushed darkness of their home, felt its icy breath on the nape of his neck. And so, he made the decision that would change everything.

Armed with a flickering flashlight and courage borrowed from the depths of his love for Amelia, her father embarked on a perilous journey into the heart of her fear. The closet, once a sanctuary of childhood dreams and secrets, had morphed into a malicious harbinger of nightmares. He knew that if he could only find the source of Amelia's torment, they could finally free her from its sinister clutches.

He yanked open the closet doors, his breath catching in his throat as he confronted the void before him. His instincts guided him, as if an invisible force was pulling him toward the truth. With each step, the resonance of fear grew louder, a symphony of terror crescendoing in his ears. He removed each item methodically, leaving no shadow unturned, until the emptiness of the closet mirrored the emptiness of their shattered hope.

The closet, once a simple wooden structure filled with Amelia's childhood toys and forgotten relics, now seemed like a gateway to an underworld. Each article of clothing, each discarded box, seemed to echo with the residual energy of the nightmares that had plagued Amelia. Her father's determination was a beacon in this sea of shadows, illuminating his path with a steadfast resolve that mirrored the fierce love he held for his daughter.

And then, his gaze fell upon the rear wall, an ominous barrier that concealed secrets beyond measure. The paneling, once securely fastened, had now shifted, exposing a hidden crawlspace. The air grew heavy with anticipation as he approached, his trembling fingers gripping the edge of that hidden passage.

Pushing aside the partition, he was struck by a gust of suffocating darkness that threatened to swallow him whole. The darkness seemed to have a life of its own, tendrils of black reaching out to pull him into the void. But he stood unwavering, a solitary figure of defiance against the unknown. With each cautious step, the walls of the crawlspace whispered their secrets, secrets that could finally unveil the truth of the Boogeyman's existence.

The crawlspace was a claustrophobic tunnel, its narrow walls closing in on him, amplifying the thudding of his heart. The air was thick with dust and decay, every breath a struggle. His flashlight flickered, casting eerie shadows that danced and twisted, playing tricks on his mind. Yet, he pressed on, driven by the thought of his daughter's suffering.

And then he saw it. There, lying amidst the shadows, was a man, his body sprawled upon a makeshift bed of desperation. Tears of fury and relief blurred his vision as he recognized the face of the intruder. For within that hidden lair, Amelia's tormentor had made his twisted den, feeding on her fear, intoxicating himself with her innocence.

The intruder's lair was a grotesque parody of a home. Old, tattered blankets and filthy pillows were strewn about, creating a nest of sorts. Empty cans and bottles littered the floor, evidence of his pathetic attempt at survival. The stench of unwashed bodies and rotten food hung heavy in the air, a nauseating reminder of the depravity that had taken root in their home.

Now, in this macabre tableau, their quarry lay sprawled, a figure consumed by his own wickedness. The twisted tendrils of his past, once locked away in the confines of his previous incarceration, had reached out once more, finding solace and sanctuary within these familiar walls. The hidden room, once concealed as an artifact of mystery, became his perverted haven, a chamber where his sinister cravings and unholy desires could be clandestinely sated.

The man's eyes, sunken and devoid of humanity, flickered open as the light from the flashlight pierced the darkness. Recognition sparked in his gaze, followed quickly by a look of malevolent glee. His lips twisted into a sneer, and he attempted to rise, but Amelia's father was faster. With a strength fueled by months of fear and anger, he lunged forward, pinning the intruder to the ground.

Rage coursed through his veins as he held the man down, his mind flashing back to every tear Amelia had shed, every sleepless night she had endured. The intruder's smug expression faltered as he realized the depth of the fury he had provoked. Amelia's father was not just fighting for his daughter; he was fighting for their family, for their home, and for the peace that had been so brutally shattered.

His mind was occupied with one question only. Why would someone do such thing to a tender soul? The demand for the truth had eluded them for so long. With every punch, the man beneath him chuckled, a sound devoid of any warmth or humor, a chilling reminder of the evil that resided within him. He tightened his grip, the urge to strike the man rising within him. But he knew that violence would not erase the horrors his daughter had faced. Instead, he focused on restraining the intruder, ensuring he could no longer inflict harm upon their family.

The authorities arrived quickly, summoned by Amelia's mother who had been anxiously waiting downstairs. They took the man away, their faces grim as they surveyed the hidden room and its ghastly contents. Amelia's father watched as they led the intruder out, his heart heavy with a mixture of relief and lingering fear.

Back upstairs, Amelia awoke to find her mother by her side, her presence a soothing balm to her frayed nerves. She didn't need to be told what had happened; the relief in her mother's eyes spoke volumes. For the first time in what felt like forever, Amelia felt a flicker of hope. The Boogeyman had been unmasked, his lair exposed, and his reign of terror brought to an end.

In the days that followed, the house was transformed. The hidden crawlspace was sealed, the closet returned to its former state as a repository of childhood memories. Amelia's parents took every measure to ensure their home was once again a place of safety and comfort. They repainted the walls, letting the fresh, clean scent of new beginnings permeate the air. They replaced the old furniture, discarding anything that carried the taint of the past.

Amelia's room, once a battleground of nightmares, became a sanctuary. Her parents filled it with light and warmth, surrounding her with love and support. They sought professional help, finding a therapist who specialized in trauma and healing. With each session, Amelia felt the weight of her fear begin to lift, replaced by a growing sense of empowerment.

The journey to recovery was not easy, nor was it swift. Nightmares still lurked at the edges of her consciousness, and the scars of her ordeal would take time to heal. But with her family by her side, Amelia faced each day with renewed strength and determination.

The Boogeyman, once an omnipresent force of terror, had been reduced to a mere memory. He no longer held power over her life, his influence shattered by the love and resilience of her family. Amelia learned to reclaim her dreams, filling her nights with visions of hope and possibility. She discovered new passions, channeling her energy into art and music, finding solace and expression in creativity.

And as the seasons changed and the world moved on, so did Amelia. She grew stronger, more confident, her spirit unbroken by the darkness that had once threatened to consume her. She knew that true security was an illusion, that the unknown would always be a part of life. But she also knew that she had the strength to face whatever challenges lay ahead, armed with the love and support of her family.

In the end, Amelia's journey was one of resilience and triumph. She had faced the Boogeyman and emerged victorious, not through violence or vengeance, but through the power of love and the unwavering support of her family. And as she stood at the threshold of her home, looking out at the world with a heart full of hope and determination, she knew that she was ready to embrace whatever the future held.

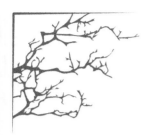

Chapter Six

AMELIA'S FATHER RECALLED the day when the Boogeyman's existence that once shrouded in secret, was abruptly dragged into the merciless light when the ear-piercing wails of alarm reverberated through the halls, summoning the authorities to confront the nightmare lurking within. The man, a monster in human skin, was swiftly apprehended, his reign of terror finally coming to an end. But the scars carved into Amelia's mind would remain, haunting her dreams for years to come.

The police had been summoned to confront a phantom, arriving with a palpable urgency in their steps, shattering the silence that had held the house captive. They had been beckoned by a family whose peaceful existence had been invaded by an entity more sinister than any mere ghost or specter. Tainted by the hushed whispers of something unspeakable, something that had seeped into their very home, an abode meant to embrace love and warmth, now defiled.

In the aftermath, Amelia's father stared at the closet, its empty depths now a reminder of the horrors they had faced. He knew that the Boogeyman would forever lurk in the shadows, ready to pounce when the veil of safety grew thin. But he would never waver in his protection, forever standing guard against the darkness that sought to claim his little girl.

And now, with a voice heavy with confession and tainted remorse, he divulged the atrocious acts committed by his filthy hands. As if painting a grotesque portrait of his transgressions, he admitted to defiling the cherubic innocence that had blossomed within Amelia's spirit. Her dolls, once conduits of imagination and joy, were violated, forever stained by his lecherous touch. Even the glimmering bracelets, delicate tokens of childhood whimsy, had been rendered corrupt, their once-pure essence desecrated by his obscenities.

But the pinnacle of his revolting admission, the dark summit of his perverted inclinations, had been his violation of her sanctity as she lay sleeping. In the ethereal veil of night, he had slithered, a serpent in the sacred garden of innocence, violating the very essence of her trust. In the hush of the twilight hours, he had perpetrated an unspeakable trespass, forever searing a wound upon her tender soul.

The revelation hung heavy in the stagnant air, like a festering tumor on the soul of this once idyllic home. As the law enforcement personnel grappled with the magnitude of the evil that had unfolded in their midst, the sinister specter of this deranged predator haunted their every thought.

In the echoing wake of this revelation, a chilling truth settled upon their trembling hearts, one that whispered of the insidiousness that lies within the souls of men. It was a truth that would forever haunt their dreams, a chilling reminder that within the folds of everyday life, a nightmare may lurk, shrouded in guile and disguised by the mask of normalcy. And it was this realization that, from that day forward, would etch itself upon their consciousness, forever tied to the nameless figure who had forever stained their home with his vile presence.

For months, this despicable predator, the Boogeyman of Thornfield, haunted their innocent daughter's dreams, threading terror and violation into the very fabric of her consciousness.

For the family, the walls of their safe haven had crumbled, exposing a depth of wickedness that defied comprehension. The remnants of comfort and tranquility, once a beacon to shield them from the horrors of the world, now lay shattered and strewn about, cruel reminders of the malevolence that had taken root in their midst. A darkness had crept into their abode, lingering like a malevolent fog, eroding their once-flourishing sense of security.

Amelia's father, once a pillar of unwavering strength, now found himself grappling with the fragile threads of his own sanity. The closet, which once served as a mere storage space, had transformed into a haunting symbol of violated trust and shattered innocence. Each time his eyes fell upon its darkened recesses, a shiver of rage and helplessness coursed through his veins, igniting a fierce determination to shield his family from any future harm.

The nights that followed were plagued with a relentless, gnawing dread. Amelia's dreams, once a sanctuary of childish wonder, had morphed into a labyrinth of terror where shadows stretched long and twisted, echoing the grotesque reality she had endured. Her sleep, once peaceful and untroubled, became a battleground where she fought against the encroaching darkness that threatened to consume her.

Her father, in his silent vigil, would often find himself standing by her bedside, watching over her with a protective gaze that bore the weight of a thousand unspoken vows. The moonlight, filtering through the curtains, cast a gentle glow on her troubled face, and he could almost see the demons she battled in her slumber. The sight tore at his heart, fueling his resolve to stand as a bulwark against the evils that lurked in the world.

The courtroom, a place meant to dispense justice and uphold truth, felt suffocating and oppressive. The air was thick with tension, as if the very walls were closing in, mirroring the claustrophobic nightmare that had engulfed their lives. Amelia's parents sat rigidly, their bodies tense with a volatile mix of shock and anger. Their eyes, once filled with joy and pride, now burned with a fierce intensity, reflecting the inner turmoil that ravaged their souls.

The proceedings were a cruel reminder of the horrors they had faced, each detail dragging them back into the abyss of despair. The man, who had once been an indistinct shadow lurking in the corners of their lives, now stood exposed, his malevolence laid bare for all to see. The gravity of his actions, the vile nature of his crimes, hung heavily in the air, a stark contrast to the mundane normalcy that the courtroom represented.

The thought of his potential release from prison was a suffocating nightmare that gnawed at their peace of mind. The mere possibility that he could walk free, unburdened by the weight of his sins, was anathema to them. It surpassed their worst fears, a gut-wrenching reality that they could scarcely comprehend. The fear of seeing his face again, of feeling his presence pollute their lives once more, was a shadow that loomed large, threatening to engulf them.

As the trial dragged on, Amelia's parents clung to each other, drawing strength from their shared pain and determination. They were bound by a common purpose, an unyielding resolve to see justice served, to ensure that the man who had shattered their world would never again have the chance to inflict such suffering. The courtroom, with its sterile decor and detached formality, became a battlefield where they waged a silent war against the darkness that had invaded their lives.

Amelia herself, though shielded from the harshest details, could sense the weight of the proceedings. Her young mind, already scarred by the horrors she had endured, struggled to make sense of the conflicting emotions that roiled within her. Fear, anger, confusion – these emotions churned in a tumultuous storm, leaving her feeling adrift and unanchored.

In the quiet moments between the chaos, she would find solace in the comforting embrace of her parents. Their unwavering presence, their unspoken vows of protection, were a lifeline that tethered her to the fragile remnants of her innocence. They were her guardians, her shield against the darkness, and in their arms, she found a semblance of peace.

The house, once a haven of laughter and love, now stood as a testament to their resilience. Each room bore the indelible marks of their ordeal, the shadows of their past lingering like specters. Yet, within those same walls, there was also a stubborn flicker of hope, a determination to rebuild, to reclaim what had been lost.

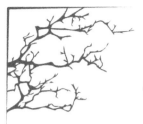

Chapter Seven

THE TRIAL, A DARK CARNIVAL in which nightmares manifested as witnesses took the stand, ended with a seemingly righteous outcome. Thirty years. An apt sentence for a monster capable of obliterating a child's innocence with each breath he took. They dared to hope that finally, justice had claimed its victory.

But life, in its twisted sense of humor, proved that justice is nothing but an elusive specter, taunting from the shadows. Bureaucratic gears began to grind, turning mercilessly, churning the promise of that righteous verdict into a cruel illusion. The Boogeyman would not face his full penance. Not even close.

Jackson Penitentiary stood as a fortress of despair, its cold and imposing walls rising high, casting a shadow over the desolate landscape. Within those oppressive confines, a darkness woven into the very fabric of its existence whispered, seeping into the minds of those unfortunate enough to call it home. The prison was a monolithic beast, its gray, weathered stones resembling the scales of some ancient creature long forgotten but still exuding an air of malevolence.

There, etched upon the walls like haunting hieroglyphs, were the whispers of countless souls, men who had long succumbed to the depths of their own depravity. Secrets lingered, festering in the recesses of every cell, staining the very air with their malignant presence. The corridors, dimly lit and perpetually damp, carried the weight of innumerable sins, a cacophony of suffering and regret echoing through their length.

But even in the midst of murderers and thieves, there was a figure that transcended the boundaries of human wickedness, casting an

28

ethereal pall over the entire institution. They called him the "Boogeyman of Thornfield," a name that sent shivers down the spines of even the most hardened criminals. It was a moniker that invoked not only fear but also an indelible mark of disgust in the hearts of those who had heard whispers of his vile tale. His true name, once whispered with reverence and used to invoke innocent terror, had long been swallowed by the abyss of his abhorrent acts.

Stories about him circulated among the inmates like urban legends passed across campfires. Some claimed he had been a harbinger of nightmares, born with darkness seeping through his veins. Whispers swore he had danced with the devil himself, casting aside any shred of humanity that might have remained. It was said that even the hardiest of criminals, men who had witnessed and perpetrated horrors of their own, quivered at the mere mention of his name.

Within those gray walls, his spectral presence loomed, an ever-present reminder of the boundaries humanity dared not cross, a living reminder of the capacity for evil that lay dormant within each soul. The Boogeyman of Thornfield was a manifestation of the deepest abyss within humanity's twisted heart, a malignant force that defied comprehension or redemption.

His cell, situated in the deepest recesses of the prison, was a place where light seemed to fear to tread. The air was thick with the scent of decay and despair, and the very walls seemed to close in, as if recoiling from the malevolence contained within. The few who had the misfortune to glimpse him reported seeing eyes that bore the weight of uncountable sins, a gaze that seemed to pierce through flesh and bone, straight into the soul.

The guards, hardened men accustomed to the darkest sides of human nature, found themselves avoiding his cell with a superstitious dread. There was an unspoken rule that no one lingered near his door, and the sound of his voice, a low and menacing rumble, was enough to send a chill through the most stoic of hearts. He was a beast among men, a predator whose hunger for innocence had not been sated, even behind bars.

The stories continued to swirl, gaining momentum with each retelling. Some claimed he could manipulate the very shadows, pulling them close like a cloak of darkness to shield him from the light. Others spoke of whispered conversations with unseen entities, bargains struck in the dead of night that ensured his vile influence extended beyond the prison walls. Whether these tales were born of truth or fear, none could say for certain, but the legend of the Boogeyman grew with each passing day.

In the dim and dreary confines of Jackson Penitentiary, his presence was a blight, a dark stain that could not be scrubbed clean. The inmates, who once considered themselves the embodiment of evil, now had a living testament to true monstrosity in their midst. They steered clear of his path, their bravado crumbling in the face of an evil that surpassed their darkest imaginations.

Amid this atmosphere of dread, the bureaucracy that held his fate in its cold, unfeeling grasp began to twist and turn. Papers shuffled, decisions were made in smoke-filled rooms far removed from the harsh reality of prison life. The promise of thirty years began to unravel, each tick of the clock eroding the foundations of what Amelia's family had believed to be justice. It was a cruel irony, a reminder that even in a place designed to contain the worst of humanity, true justice could be a fleeting dream.

For Amelia and her family, the news of his impending early release was a blow that reopened barely healed wounds. The thought of him walking free, breathing the same air as they did, was a nightmare that eclipsed even their darkest memories. The world outside, with its bright sunshine and bustling life, seemed a mockery of their suffering, a stark contrast to the shadow that had permanently marked their existence.

Amelia's parents, who had fought so fiercely for justice, now found themselves grappling with a sense of helplessness. The legal battles that had once filled them with a righteous fury now seemed like hollow victories, overshadowed by the realization that true safety might forever elude them. The Boogeyman's shadow loomed large, a constant presence in their thoughts, a reminder of the evil that could never be fully contained.

And so, life moved on in a cruel parody of normalcy. The sun rose and set, the seasons changed, and yet, for Amelia and her family, time seemed to stand still, trapped in a loop of fear and uncertainty. The hope that had once burned brightly within them now flickered weakly, like a candle struggling against a relentless wind.

Jackson Penitentiary, with its cold, gray walls and air thick with despair, remained a stark testament to the limits of human justice. Within its confines, the Boogeyman of Thornfield continued to exist, a dark reminder of the evil that lurks within the human heart. And beyond those walls, the family he had once terrorized struggled to rebuild their lives, haunted by the knowledge that true justice might always remain just out of reach.

Chapter Eight

THE ARYANS, A GANG that reeked of darkness and sported tattoos of hate, gathered in the shadows of the penitentiary showers. The air was thick with the stench of mildew and stale sweat, the dim lighting casting eerie shadows that danced across the cold, damp tiles. They knew what lay beneath the façade of the man they called The Boogeyman—a monster, a predator. The whispers slithered among them, like venomous serpents coiling around their very souls, as if the syllables themselves could draw blood and seek justice. "Child molester," they hissed, their words laced with a palpable venom that seemed to poison the very air they breathed.

The air hummed with anticipation, a charged energy that crackled like a live wire, setting the atmosphere alight with a macabre excitement. The steel showerheads, hanging like metallic sentinels, glistened under the flickering fluorescent lights, almost salivating at the impending dance of retribution. For The Boogeyman, this was no ordinary stumble into a gang's crosshairs. It was an immersion into pure hell, a descent into the abyss where demons feasted upon the flesh and bones of the damned. The walls, slick with moisture, seemed to close in, amplifying the tension that hung heavy in the air.

The gangsters, driven by a twisted sense of justice, reveled in this macabre theater. They had become the choreographers of their own twisted ballet, their blades the elegant dancers upon this atrocious stage. The clang of metal against tile resonated through the shower room, a sinister overture to the symphony of violence that was about to unfold. The air filled with a symphony of metal cutting through resistance, punctuating the wet, murky stillness with the sickening thud of flesh meeting steel.

The Boogeyman, his body nothing more than a canvas of suffering and sin, twisted and writhed in a grotesque interpretation of life itself. Each blade slashed and tore, becoming a conductor of pain and retribution. His skin, once taut and menacing, now hung in shreds, a testament to the fury unleashed upon him. The man, dripping not only with water but with the weight of his sins, became an effigy of their hatred. The Aryans found perverse solace in this bloody punishment, their fury feeding upon his torment.

His screams, anguished and primal, filled the prison halls—an unholy melody of suffering that echoed through the walls, like a haunting requiem for his desecration of innocence. The prisoners, desperate to escape the reality of their confinement, listened in hushed awe. Some closed their eyes, savoring the symphony with a sick voyeurism, while others exchanged malevolent smiles—an unspoken acknowledgment that there was justice in this world, twisted as it may be.

When the music of blades finally quieted, the Aryans stood back, their blunt instruments of justice glinting with a satiated hunger. The silence enveloped the scene, broken only by the rhythm of the pedophile's ragged breaths. His once formidable demeanor had crumbled, reduced to a trembling heap of broken humanity. Blood pooled around him, mingling with the soapy water to form a gruesome tapestry of red and white, swirling down the drain as if to cleanse the area of the evil that had tainted it.

The gangsters, their faces a tapestry of satisfaction, turned away from the tableau of brutality they had orchestrated. They left the showers, stepping over the detritus of their retribution with a subtle swagger. In their wake, The Boogeyman of Thornfield lay broken and defeated, serving as a grotesque reminder of the darkness that dwelled within the human heart.

In the eyes of the Aryans, they had enacted a twisted justice, a vigilante act that punished the unrepentant. But as the echoes of his agonized screams faded into the unforgiving abyss of the prison, one question lingered—had they truly eradicated the beast, or had they merely added their own darkness to an already sinister world?

The Boogeyman, as they called him, was a man of twisted desires. The kind that surface in the darkest corners of the human psyche, lurking in the shadows of forbidden dreams. He preyed on the innocent, stirring fear and leaving devastation in his wake. The kind of monster that could only flourish in the underbelly of a world turned upside down.

But on that fateful day, as hatred and rage converged, the Aryans sought to rid their prison of this abomination. They saw themselves as righteous warriors, purging the impurity that stained their ranks. With sharpened blades, they descended upon him like vengeful angels, delivering a hailstorm of relentless slashes and punctures. Their movements were almost ritualistic, each thrust of the blade a sacrament in their dark liturgy of vengeance.

Each strike was intended to be fatal, to rid the world of this despicable pedophile. But fate, with its own twisted sense of irony, had other plans. The Boogeyman clung to life, gasping for breath in a sea of crimson. His body, once recognizable, now a grotesque mosaic of torn flesh and shattered bones. A morbid masterpiece, painted in hues of pain and suffering, laid out for all to see.

The aftermath was a scene of eerie quiet, the echoes of violence slowly dissipating like smoke in the wind. The floor, slick with blood and water, reflected the grotesque image of a man who had once been a terror to the innocent. The prison walls, silent witnesses to countless atrocities, now bore witness to this latest act of retribution. The shadows seemed to grow longer, as if stretching to cover the horrors that had been unveiled in their midst.

In the bowels of Jackson Penitentiary, justice had taken on a monstrous form, and the lines between right and wrong had blurred beyond recognition. The Boogeyman, though beaten and broken, still breathed, his existence a testament to the persistence of evil. And as the Aryans walked away, their dark deed etched into the annals of prison lore, the prison itself seemed to sigh, as if acknowledging that in the end, no one truly escapes the darkness that lies within.

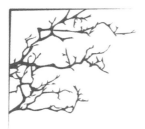

Chapter Nine

THE ROOKIE GUARD, HIS silence etched in fear-soaked memories, stared at the gruesome sight before him, his eyes widening in sheer disbelief. The showers, once a haven for brief respite from the abominable darkness that permeated the prison, now became the very manifestation of that darkness itself. The place where every sinner was supposed to wash off their sins at the beginning of each day turned to the most horrific place in the prison. The flickering fluorescent lights cast a sickly glow on the scene, illuminating the crimson chaos that painted the tiles. The Boogeyman, a name whispered in terrified murmurs throughout the penitentiary, lay broken and forlorn, his body twisted in a grotesque dance of pain and suffering. His limbs, contorted and askew, spoke of the violent ballet that had played out mere moments before.

The pool of blood, a macabre masterpiece of crimson art, seemed to mock him, each droplet an echo of the horrors that had unfolded within these walls. It spread slowly, inexorably, like a dark omen creeping across the white tiles. But what held his gaze, what refused to release his trembling soul, was the sight of The Boogeyman still clinging to life. Against all odds, against the very laws of nature, this monster still breathed. His chest rose and fell in shallow, erratic rhythms, each breath a testament to his indomitable will to survive.

The guards, their minds awash with a chilling cocktail of fear and loathing, exchanged glances that conveyed the unspeakable truth they dared not utter. It would be so simple to abandon this abomination, to allow him to die alone in the perverse shadows of the prison walls. The walls seemed to close in, amplifying the weight of their unspoken thoughts. But the Warden, a man condemned to a lifetime of overseeing this hellish realm, knew the true horrors that awaited them should news of this ghastly incident spread beyond their realm.

Without a moment's hesitation, the Warden bellowed orders, his voice a thunderous bolt of authority in the midst of chaos. The sound reverberated through the damp, echoing halls, shaking the guards from their stupor. The guards, their hearts pounding in their chests, scooped up the mangled remains of The Boogeyman, his body both a testament to human frailty and an embodiment of inhuman strength. Blood stained their hands, seeping into the very fabric of their psyches, forever branding them with the mark of unspeakable horror.

The race against time began, the shriek of sirens blending with the palpable dread that coiled around them all. The hallways, once a monotonous gray, now seemed like a nightmarish labyrinth, each turn fraught with urgency. The local emergency room, a sanctuary of salvation for the mortally wounded, stood as their only beacon of hope. But even as they stumbled through those sterile corridors, the life slipping from The Boogeyman's broken form before their very eyes, a lingering doubt etched itself in the hearts of all who bore witness to this calamity. There was no saving him. Not from this.

Surgery, a dance between life and death performed by skilled hands, laid bare the machinations of fate. The blood flowed freely, a river of life coursing through the desperate veins of a man teetering on the precipice of eternity. The operating room, bathed in harsh, sterile light, became a battleground where surgeons fought a relentless war against the encroaching darkness. And yet, in the face of the impossible, The Boogeyman defied all expectations. He died, not once but multiple times on that sterile operating table. Each time, the desperate surge of panic swelled, the hope of salvation eroded beneath the relentless tide of reality.

The surgeons, their hands guided by a grim determination, fought a losing battle against the vortex of impossibility. Death hung in the air, its fetid breath mingling with the antiseptic sting of the room. The rhythmic beeping of the monitors seemed to slow, each pause an eternity, as if time itself held its breath. And yet, as the final heartbeat echoed like a desperate plea for mercy, The Boogeyman reemerged from the abyss of eternity.

It defied reason, logic, and the whispers of uncertainty that dwelled within the darkest corners of the human psyche. The guards, silent witnesses to this impossible resurrection, exchanged glances once more, their eyes now filled with a mingling cocktail of horror and awe. There was no way he should be alive, no logical explanation for this perverse dance with mortality. Their gazes, once hardened by the realities of prison life, now betrayed a vulnerability, a crack in their stoic facades.

As The Boogeyman's eyes fluttered open, fragments of his shattered consciousness pieced together the remnants of tortured memory that remained. His vision, blurry and unfocused, gradually sharpened, revealing the stark white of the hospital room ceiling above him. The darkness that had consumed him now seemed woven into the very fabric of his existence. Every breath, every heartbeat, a testament to the sinister force that animated his wretched being. And thus, like a tortured wraith, he rose from that operating table, ready to continue his reign of terror, leaving behind a room drowning in an ocean of blood and unanswered questions.

The sterile, antiseptic air of the operating room seemed to grow colder, the chill seeping into the bones of all present. The surgeons, their faces etched with disbelief and exhaustion, could only watch as the impossible unfolded before their eyes. The Boogeyman, a creature of nightmare given flesh, had defied death itself. The fluorescent lights flickered momentarily, as if the very fabric of reality shuddered at his revival.

In the bowels of Jackson Penitentiary, a new chapter of horror had been written. The Boogeyman, though beaten and broken, still breathed, his existence a testament to the persistence of evil. His survival, a grotesque mockery of the justice the Aryans had sought to impose, loomed like a dark specter over the prison. And as the guards escorted him back, their minds heavy with the weight of what they had witnessed, the prison itself seemed to sigh, as if acknowledging that in the end, no one truly escapes the darkness that lies within.

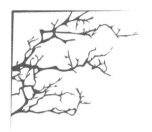

Chapter Ten

WORD OF HIS SURVIVAL spread like wildfire through the prison's whispered tales. Fear and curiosity danced hand in hand, swirling like a dark tempest through the labyrinthine halls of Jackson Penitentiary. The inmates, hardened by their own sins, found their own twisted fascination ignited by the resurrection of this infamous specter. The Boogeyman, once thought vanquished, was now a prisoner amongst prisoners, a living ghost in their midst. The authorities, facing a pressure cooker of violence ready to explode, had no choice but to yield. They whisked him away, burying him under the umbrella of protective custody, rendering him a forgotten ghost in the prison's depths.

Jackson Penitentiary held many secrets, but none quite as dark as the murky depths of the Boogeyman's past. His presence lingered like a shadow in the corners of the prison, a silent reminder of the malevolence that humans can harbor. He remained locked away, a specter tormenting not only the souls shackled within those grim confines but haunting the imagination of the world outside. The walls of his cell seemed to pulse with the dark energy of his deeds, absorbing the whispers of his name that still circulated among the inmates. His was a tale left untold, for fear that to uncover it would be to unleash a malevolence that could never be contained.

So, the Boogeyman of Thornfield stood, a specter of iniquity, forgotten by those who dared to forget, and forever etched into the darkest corners of Jackson Penitentiary – a place where whispers transformed into screams, and lost innocence became an eternal torment. The silence around his cell was thick, almost tangible, as if the air itself was afraid to move too freely in his presence. The other inmates, even the most brutal and unrepentant, steered clear of his confines, their fear a palpable force that only served to isolate him further.

It was a gray and dreary morning when the news of The Boogeyman's survival reached Amelia, weaving its tendrils of terror around her weary heart. The clouds seemed to gather in sinister formations, casting a pall over the world she once believed to be safe. The sun, once a steadfast beacon of hope, now appeared feeble and distant, its rays unable to penetrate the darkness that encased her soul. Her heart clenched with an icy grip, each beat a painful reminder of the terror that once shadowed her existence.

Amelia's mind flashed back to that bleak courtroom, the walls echoing with the cries of her grief-stricken heart. The conviction had seemed like a victory, a triumph of justice over evil. The Boogeyman, that vile predator, had been found guilty for his heinous acts. The chains of his wickedness had seemed unbreakable, destined to keep him imprisoned in the depths of his own malevolence. And yet, like a devilish phoenix rising from the ashes, he had somehow escaped his just deserts.

Dread juxtaposed with anger within Amelia's fragile frame, intertwining to form an overwhelming cocktail of emotions. How could this be? How could fate be so callously cruel? His survival was a grotesque slap in the face, a savage reminder that darkness could not be vanquished so easily. In Amelia's mind, the world shifted on its axis, forever turning her towards him, like a baying hound on the scent of its prey.

Her nightmares, once banished to the recesses of her mind, now resurfaced with malicious intent. Visions of his face, twisted by malice, invaded her dreams, suffocating her with their suffused malevolence. As she sought solace within the safe confines of her once-secure home, every creak of the floorboards sent shivers down her spine. The shadows danced with an eerie vivacity, whispering menacing secrets that only she could hear. The comforting embrace of her familiar surroundings now felt like a deceptive trap, the darkness seeming to press in from every corner.

The news of his survival had awakened a dormant terror within Amelia, forcing her to confront the demons she had sought to bury. Every step she took, every breath she drew, felt like an unsteady dance on a razor's edge. She was walking a tightrope between fate and despair, her heart raw with a mix of fear and determination. The world around her seemed to lose its vibrant hues, everything tinged with a gray uncertainty that reflected her inner turmoil.

Amelia could not let him win. She would not allow him to cast his wicked spell upon her world once more. With renewed purpose burning in her veins, she set forth on a perilous quest for justice. No matter the cost, no matter the toll it would take on her fragile psyche, she would not rest until The Boogeyman was once again behind bars, his sinister grip on her world extinguished forever. She steeled herself against the memories that threatened to engulf her, transforming her fear into a weapon of resolve.

Her days became a relentless pursuit, a tireless march through the bureaucracy of the justice system. Each meeting with lawyers, each conversation with authorities, was a battle fought with the shadow of his evil looming over her. The fire of determination in her eyes never dimmed, even as exhaustion etched lines into her face. Her spirit, though battered, remained unbroken, fueled by the need to see him confined once more.

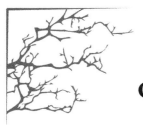

Chapter Eleven

THE DARKNESS THAT CONSUMED the Boogeyman of Thornfield was far from extinguished. It prowled his very being, igniting an insatiable hunger for destruction that no prison cell could contain. The guards whispered among themselves, exchanging stories of his eerie silence, the chilling absence of remorse that lingered in his eyes. The aura around him was palpable, a malevolent force that seemed to distort the very air, making it thick and oppressive. Every time he passed, a shiver of unease rippled through the ranks, a silent acknowledgment of the monster who lurked within.

Amelia, older now and scarred by the events of her past, clung to the fragments of her shattered innocence. She had built a life, molded from the fractured pieces of her childhood, yet the Boogeyman loomed in the shadows, a constant reminder of the evil that still thrived within the world. Each day was a struggle to maintain her equilibrium, to forge a future unmarred by the horrors that once claimed her. The echo of her torment resonated through her dreams, a silent scream that refused to fade, no matter how far she ran from its source.

It was a frigid winter's night when the prison walls quivered with an unspoken anticipation. Whispers meandered through the corridors, swirling in a frenzy of unease. The Boogeyman, it was said, had begun to speak in his sleep, his sinister mutterings echoing through the hollow halls of Jackson Penitentiary. His voice, once a weapon of terror, now seeped into the darkness, infecting the very stones with his malignant essence. The guards, their faces etched with lines of fear and exhaustion, exchanged glances, their unease growing with each passing night.

Amelia's curiosity seeped through her weary bones. She had buried her memories deep, setting them ablaze in the recesses of her mind. But the haunting whispers awakened something dormant within her, a defiant flame that refused to be extinguished by time or distance. The news of his nocturnal ramblings stirred a resolve within her, a need to confront the demon that had once stolen her childhood. She knew that facing him was the only way to reclaim the parts of herself that still lay shackled in the past.

As the prison guards grappled with the perverse enigma that was the Boogeyman, Amelia and her parents made their way to the depths of Jackson Penitentiary. They navigated the labyrinthine corridors, her breath forming small clouds of determination in the frigid air. Each step was a testament to her courage, the culmination of years spent in therapy, fortifying her spirit and transforming her into a warrior intent on facing the horrors that had shaped her existence. Her parents, their faces drawn with concern and resolve, walked beside her, their presence a pillar of strength in the encroaching darkness.

In the bowels of the penitentiary, they found him. Her captor from the days of her youth, his pallid complexion and sunken eyes were a ghastly testament to the monster he had become. The very sight of him churned her insides, a tempest of anguish and fury. His presence was an affront to the life she had painstakingly rebuilt, a reminder of the innocence he had stolen. The cell, cold and dank, seemed to pulse with the dark energy of his malevolence, each shadow a fragment of the horror he embodied.

As she stared into his vacant eyes, Amelia's voice, once silenced by the terror that had stolen her innocence, rose in a crescendo of defiance. She confronted him with a torrent of questions, each word a blade that pierced the feeble mask he had woven around himself. Her voice, trembling yet resolute, demanded answers, demanded justice. The room seemed to hold its breath, the air crackling with the raw power of her confrontation.

But the Boogeyman remained silent, his twisted lips curling into a sinister smile. He reveled in the torment he had caused, the scars he had etched upon Amelia's soul. Instead of answers, he offered her a macabre symphony of whispers, a symphony that threatened to drown her in the sea of her own fears. His eyes, devoid of humanity, gleamed with a perverse satisfaction, feeding off the pain he saw reflected in hers.

In that suffocating darkness, Amelia understood. The Boogeyman was not to be defeated by confrontation or revenge. He fed on the fear he sowed, the power he held over those who dared to challenge him. A wickedness like his could only be extinguished by the light of hope, the echo of love that persisted in even the most desolate corners of the human heart. She realized that his true defeat lay not in his destruction, but in her refusal to let his darkness define her.

With a newfound resolve, Amelia turned her back on the Boogeyman of Thornfield. She refused to let him consume her presence or define her existence. As they walked away, she felt the heavy weight of his malevolence slip from her shoulders, replaced by the gentle touch of her parents' arms. Their support, unwavering and warm, enveloped her like a shield against the cold tendrils of her past. Each step away from his cell was a step towards her own liberation, towards a future untainted by his shadow.

In the dim light of the prison's exit, Amelia took a deep breath, the frigid air filling her lungs with a sense of renewal. She was not the broken child he had once known. She was a survivor, a beacon of resilience and strength. The Boogeyman might have cast a long shadow, but she had found the light within herself to banish it. And with that light, she would forge a new path, one that led away from the darkness and towards a future defined by hope and love.

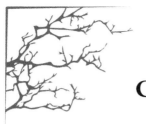

Chapter Twelve

ISOLATION BECAME HIS new companion, a haunting specter that no longer only scared others but also enveloped his own existence. The days blended into nights, his once vibrant spirit now dimmed by the crushing weight of despair. No bars or locks could contain the demons festering inside him, the ones he had so freely unleashed upon others. The cell that confined him became a dark cocoon, wrapping tighter around him with each passing day, suffocating any remnants of the man he once was.

Days turned into months, marking the passage of time within his windowless cell. He became a ghost within a ghost town, fading further into obscurity with each passing day. His identity, once a source of twisted pride, now eroded under the relentless tide of time and isolation. The silence of his cell was punctuated only by the distant echoes of the prison, a reminder of the life teeming just beyond his reach.

But even in the depths of solitude, the Boogeyman of Thornfield was not free from the other demons that haunted these prison walls. Night after night, he would lay in his cell, his mind enraptured by the memories of his crimes. Images of Amelia's angelic face, twisted by his vile acts, flashed before his eyes like a perverted slideshow. He pleasured himself in his cell, his twisted memories feeding his depraved desires. The recollection of her innocence, violated and tainted by his actions, became his nightly ritual, a dark testament to his unrepentant nature.

The other convicts, murderous animals screaming for blood, taunted and threatened him. In the land of monsters, anything goes. Yet, even amidst the jeers and threats, he found a perverse solace in his memories, a sanctuary within the chaos. He had taken delight in her fear, reveled in the power he held over her fragile spirit. He had been a shadow that lurked in the corners of her existence, a nightmare that refused to dissipate with the morning light. And now, in the desolation of his prison cell, he slept like a baby, unburdened by the weight of his atrocities.

But it wasn't just the memories that aroused him. It was the knowledge that somewhere out there, he had left a trail of shattered lives in his wake. The parents who would never truly know peace, the child whose innocence had been forever stolen. He was a monster, an aberration that society could not comprehend or forgive. His name, once synonymous with terror and innocence lost, had been buried beneath the weight of his abhorrent acts.

He was the man they called the "Boogeyman of Thornfield," a moniker that invoked a mixture of fear and disgust in the hearts of those who had heard his vile tale. Amelia, just a child, had been the unfortunate recipient of his heinous crimes. Time, like a merciless warden, held its scepter high and carved its mark upon the walls of Thornfield, etching the memory of his deeds into the fabric of the prison.

The overcrowded penal system, its hungry maw devouring those unfortunate enough to fall into its clutches, became a catalyst for change. Good behavior, a twisted irony considering its bearer, granted him a path towards a tainted redemption. He ascended to the position of trustee, a vulture given wings within the crumbling confines of his cage. And so, with barely three years behind bars, the man was ripped from the grasp of prison life. The bars that had once confined him were now a distant memory, the cell that had once been his prison now an empty husk.

Parole was extended as if it were a gift, an ink-stained document that sealed his freedom. Yet, the question lingered in the shadows, staining the hearts of those who knew his chilling tale—was justice truly served? The world outside, unaware of the darkness that had been unleashed once more, continued its ceaseless march forward. But for those who remembered, for those who bore the scars of his malevolence, the shadow of the Boogeyman of Thornfield would never truly fade.

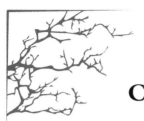

Chapter Thirteen

AN ABYSS OF DISBELIEF swallowed their hearts whole when news reached their ears. Only three years served. Three measly years behind granite walls adorned with ceramic angels and hollow motivational sayings, meant to soothe but failing miserably in their task. "Good behavior," they claimed, those words dripping with sickening irony, like venomous whispers of a system that had callously overlooked the depths of their daughter's suffering.

Amelia had believed herself liberated from the clutches of the Boogeyman when justice seemed to have prevailed. Yet now, with his premature release, she found herself once again ensnared in the malevolent web of his influence. The dark recesses of her consciousness, once tentatively opening to thoughts of healing, now pulsed with a sinister anticipation of impending doom. Shadows lengthened and twisted, every corner harboring the potential for the Boogeyman's return, like a predator waiting to pounce upon its unsuspecting prey.

Her parents, straining against the urge to unleash primal screams of rage and despair, were swept away on a relentless tide of injustice. In that moment, their daughter's pain was relegated to a footnote in the bureaucratic shuffle, a trauma that gnawed relentlessly at her psyche while the wheels of the indifferent system turned.

Free once more, the Boogeyman emerged from the shadow of his prison cell, a specter of malice and unchecked evil. Thornfield, once a prison where nightmares were contained, now breathed with a renewed malevolence, its grim history resurfacing like a festering wound reopened upon an unsuspecting world. The town recoiled in horror, haunted anew by the specter they had hoped to forget, a specter that now roamed free among them, a living embodiment of their worst fears realized.

Amelia's parents clung to each other, their hands intertwined in a white-knuckled grip, their faces drained of color under the weight of their anguish. From that moment forward, they vowed to stand as sentinels for their daughter, drawing courage from the depths of their shattered souls, even as their hearts fractured into a thousand jagged pieces.

Their fight was not just for Amelia but for every innocent soul crushed beneath the suffocating embrace of an unjust system. The Boogeyman's release marked not an end but a rallying cry against the shadows that threatened to engulf them all. His name, etched in infamy upon their family's history, would not silence their voices or dull their resolve.

Reality, as it unfolded in its cruel twists and turns, bore terrors far more brutal than any conjured by the imagination. As the machinery of a broken system ground forward, their daughter's pain became an indelible scar upon their souls, a wound that bled with the agony of a thousand injustices, staining their lives until their final breaths.

Amelia, now older but forever marked by the atrocities inflicted upon her by the Boogeyman, had believed herself safe when justice seemed to have been served. A fleeting sigh of relief had echoed through the town, a brief respite from the nightmare that had plagued her existence. But fate, in its capricious dance, had other plans.

In a bewildering twist of fate, Amelia's tormentor was granted parole a mere three years into his sentence. The justice system, often blind and indifferent, had released the monster back into the world, leaving Amelia to grapple with a surge of anxiety that threatened to consume her whole.

Every step she took was now burdened by the oppressive weight of paranoia. Shadows elongated and contorted into the grotesque form of her nemesis, lurking around every corner, hiding in plain sight. Faces of strangers took on sinister expressions, their smiles twisted into malevolent grins. Even the whispers of the wind carried echoes of his sinister voice, taunting her, haunting her, a reminder that the Boogeyman had never truly left. He had become an omnipresent phantom, a malevolent specter that haunted her every waking moment.

In this maelstrom of fear, Amelia's fragile psyche began to unravel. Sleep, once an escape from the horrors of her waking life, now became a treacherous landscape fraught with terrors. Nightmares clawed at the edges of her consciousness, twisting reality into grotesque shapes that mirrored the horrors of her past. Each night she would awaken in a cold sweat, her heart pounding in her chest like the ominous beat of a funeral drum.

In the light of day, Amelia's dread took on myriad forms. Every passing glance, every whispered conversation, seemed laden with hidden meanings and unspoken threats. The world outside continued its relentless march, unaware of the storm brewing within her, a tempest of fear and despair that threatened to engulf her whole.

She was adrift in a sea of uncertainty, a lone ship battered by the relentless waves of paranoia and dread. The Boogeyman's release had torn open old wounds, exposing her to the raw agony of past traumas. Her fragile sanity, already fractured by the Boogeyman's depravity, teetered on the brink of collapse.

Yet, amidst the turmoil, a flicker of defiance ignited within Amelia's soul. She refused to surrender to the shadows that sought to consume her. With each breath, she summoned the courage to face the day, to confront the demons that haunted her. The fight for justice was far from over, and Amelia would not rest until the Boogeyman was held accountable for the devastation he had wrought upon her life and countless others.

In the heart of darkness, where nightmares lurked and fears took tangible form, Amelia stood as a beacon of resilience. She was a survivor, forged in the crucible of unspeakable trauma, her spirit tempered by the fires of adversity. The battle against the Boogeyman was a battle for her very soul, a test of courage and perseverance in the face of unimaginable horror.

And as she faced each day with unwavering determination, Amelia drew strength from the love and support of her parents, their unwavering presence a bulwark against the storm. Together, they would navigate the treacherous waters ahead, united in their quest for justice and their refusal to be silenced by the darkness that threatened to engulf them all.

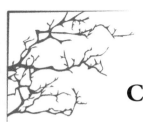

Chapter Fourteen

THE DESCENT INTO MADNESS unfurled like a twisted tableau, drawing unwanted attention that rippled through crowded public spaces. Amelia's cries of terror echoed like desperate pleas, piercing the veil of normalcy that surrounded her. Concerned murmurs swirled in eddies of sympathy and fear, an ominous gathering storm that hovered over her tormented soul. Her parents, heartbroken witnesses to their daughter's unraveling, found themselves cornered by a painful decision, their options narrowing with each passing day.

The sanitarium loomed on the horizon, a stark institution of white walls and sterile halls that promised treatment amidst its bleak corridors. For Amelia and her distraught family, it represented both a beacon of hope and a plunge into the unknown depths of despair. In their desperation, they hesitated on the brink of this final recourse, knowing it could mean condemning Amelia to a fate not unlike her own personal purgatory.

Until the day they could make a definitive choice, Amelia's mind teetered on the precipice of sanity, her world a nightmarish labyrinth of fear and uncertainty. Whether it was the lingering specter of the Boogeyman or the phantoms birthed from her shattered psyche, the horrors of Thornfield refused to loosen their grip. Amelia, caught in the relentless tug-of-war between reality and delusion, harbored a primal fear that the Boogeyman would return to claim her once more.

Amelia's parents, grappling with their daughter's agonizing descent, sought refuge in the promises of modern medicine. The doctors at the sanitarium prescribed an array of medications, each pill a fragile lifeline meant to dull her pain and quell the relentless storm of hallucinations.

Yet, even in the medicated haze that clouded her senses, the Boogeyman persisted, an insidious presence that mocked the efficacy of their efforts.

Days blurred into weeks, and weeks into months, but Amelia's torment showed no signs of abating. She navigated through life like a ghostly apparition, her vacant eyes betraying the deep-seated terror that gnawed at her fragile mind. Nights became a battleground where sleep eluded her grasp, leaving her tangled in sheets soaked with sweat, her heart racing like a frantic drumbeat in the darkness. In her desperate bid to ward off sleep, Amelia sought solace in the dangerous embrace of Adderall and crack cocaine, substances that ensnared her body in their merciless grip, offering temporary respite from the relentless nightmares that plagued her.

Her parents, ravaged by helplessness and grief, watched with anguished hearts as their beloved daughter slipped further into the abyss. Their once tranquil home became a battlefield, where Amelia's tortured screams shattered the fragile peace they had fought so hard to preserve. The Boogeyman's malevolent presence now permeated every corner of their existence, casting shadows that stretched across their sanity like creeping tendrils of darkness.

With heavy hearts burdened by the weight of their daughter's suffering, they made the agonizing decision to readmit Amelia to the sanitarium that had briefly sheltered her before. It was a last-ditch effort, a desperate plea for the doctors to unlock the mysteries of her tormented mind and restore some semblance of peace to her shattered world. The stark walls of her room, once a temporary haven, now closed in around her like silent sentinels, bearing witness to the harrowing journey she embarked upon anew through the labyrinth of her fractured psyche.

In the depths of her isolation, where the boundaries between reality and hallucination blurred into an indistinct haze, Amelia fought a battle that defied conventional understanding. Each day was a fragile truce in the war waged against her own mind, a relentless struggle to reclaim the fragments of her sanity from the clutches of madness. Every day, it was different for her. Some days she would feel like she had finally gotten over it and some days, her mind would drag her into the deepest pits of her sorrow. Her parents, stalwart in their devotion despite the crushing weight of despair, clung to a flicker of hope that somewhere within the labyrinth of her tortured psyche, their daughter would find the strength to emerge victorious against the demons that threatened to consume her whole.

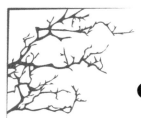

Chapter Fifteen

AS FOR AMELIA'S FATHER, he had reached his breaking point. Every time he looked at his daughter, he saw the pain in her eyes, the deep scars etched into her soul. He carried the weight of his failure like a never-ending burden, his guilt gnawing at him night and day. How could he ever forgive himself for not believing her? For not staying by her side, being the pillar of strength she so desperately needed?

Restlessness plagued him as much as it did Amelia. Each of her nightmares became his own, every scream reverberating through his heart. The thought that a monster had tormented his little girl while he slept soundly in the room next door was an agony he could not escape. Night after night, he lay awake, replaying the moments he dismissed her fears, convincing himself it was just childish imagination. How could he have been so blind, so foolish?

He felt like a failure, a father who had let his guard down, allowing his daughter to be consumed by terror. The Boogeyman, once a figment of nightmares, had manifested into a very real threat, and he had done nothing to stop it. The shame of his inaction was a heavy cloak he could not shed. Each time Amelia's fragile form trembled with fear, he saw the consequences of his disbelief and the depths of her suffering.

Now, with news of the Boogeyman of Thornfield's release on parole, his desperation took on a whole new level. The rage simmering within him threatened to boil over. For months, he and a group of other fathers in the town had been quietly searching for the Boogeyman's new residence, their determination fueled by a vengeance that could no longer be contained. These men were the protectors, the ones who vowed to shield their children from the horrors of the world. And now, they saw an opportunity to seek vigilante justice, to ensure that the nightmare haunting Thornfield would never threaten their families again.

Amelia's father was at the forefront of this pursuit, driven by a need to atone for his perceived failures. He could no longer sit idly by, consumed by guilt and regret. The Boogeyman had to be stopped, and he was prepared to do whatever it took to protect his daughter and the children of Thornfield. The thought of the Boogeyman roaming free, capable of inflicting more pain, was a reality he refused to accept.

In the silence of the night, as Amelia found fleeting moments of peace, her father's resolve hardened. He knew that his redemption lay in his actions, in the steps he took to ensure that no other child would suffer as his daughter had. The weight of his failure was a constant reminder, a driving force pushing him towards the path of justice. The monster may have once lurked in the shadows of his daughter's room, but now, he would become the hunter, seeking to banish the Boogeyman from their lives forever.

For months, he and a group of other fathers in the town had been quietly searching for the Boogeyman's new residence, their determination fueled by a rage that could no longer be contained. These men were the protectors, the ones who vowed to shield their children from the horrors of the world. And now, they saw an opportunity to seek vigilante justice, to ensure that the nightmare haunting Thornfield would never threaten their families again.

It was the dead of night, the witching hour, where shadows danced like specters and the air crackled with a palpable sense of dread. Amelia's father was among them, a hardened man driven by the primal instinct to protect his kin. Eight other fathers, united by a shared terror that had consumed their lives, stood alongside him. Determined, they embarked on a journey that would forever alter the course of their existence.

The place reeked of decay, and ominous shadows stretched across the overgrown lawn like the fingers of a supernatural entity, reaching for your very soul. This was it – their chance to confront the darkness that had marred their lives for far too long.

Amelia's father stood at the front of the group, his heart pounding in his chest. A flicker of fear danced in the recesses of his mind, threatening to extinguish his resolve. But he quelled it, determined not to back down this time. He stepped forward, a man on a precipice, summoning his remaining strength.

In the heart of Thornfield, a place suffused with whispers of the unspeakable, they made their move. With a nod of silent agreement, the fathers descended upon the house like avenging angels. The door trembled under the weight of anticipation as they unleashed their collective fury, shattering the fragile barrier that separated them from their nemesis. With a deafening crash, they entered the room, ravenous beasts converging upon their prey.

There he stood, the personification of their darkest nightmares incarnate. The Boogeyman, caught in the very act of attempting to escape through the bedroom window, froze, his eyes wide with terror, realizing that his reign of terror was finally coming to an end. But mercy was a luxury they could not afford, demons had no place in their world.

With unbridled rage coursing through their veins, the men surrounded him, feral hands raining down upon his wretched form. Blow after blow, the echoes of vengeance reverberated through the once-quiet room, the symphony of brutality punctuated only by the agonizing gasps of their prey. Blood pooled on the floor, mingling with the darkness that had consumed Thornfield for far too long.

But their wrath knew no bounds; they sought to immolate the very core of evil that tainted their lives. A broom handle, splintered into two crude halves, became their instrument of retribution. Brutally and mercilessly, they thrust it upward, possessing a grim determination to deliver justice in the most visceral manner possible. The Boogeyman succumbed to the torment, his fate forever sealed in a macabre act of poetic justice.

With their mission complete, they turned their attention to the citadel of wickedness that had housed their tormentor. Flames erupted within the hellish confine, greedily consuming any remnants of darkness that clung to the walls. The inferno roared triumphantly, its fiery tongues licking at the night sky, illuminating the grim faces of those who had wrested Thornfield from the clutches of despair.

Under the cloak of the night, they dispersed, each father carrying the weight of their shared secret, forever bound by the terrors they had vanquished. Amelia's father, eyes weary but resolute, glanced backward once, daring to glimpse the raging conflagration that had overtaken the place that had unleashed untold horrors upon their lives. And as he strode into the darkness, a ray of hope pierced through the lingering shadows, promising a new dawn free from the clutches of the unspeakable terror that the Boogeyman had wrought.

For Thornfield would forever carry the scars of their battle, a testament to the resilience of the human spirit and the lengths a person would go to protect those they loved. The townspeople had faced the embodiment of their worst nightmares and emerged victorious, though at a great cost. The horrors they had witnessed would forever haunt their dreams, but they had faced the darkness head-on, sparing no mercy for the demons that dwelled within their midst.

In the following days, Thornfield slowly began to rebuild. The townspeople, though wary and forever changed, found solace in the knowledge that the Boogeyman was no more. The fathers, now bound by their shared ordeal, formed an unspoken pact to protect their community from any future threats. They became the silent sentinels, ever watchful, ever ready to confront any darkness that might dare to return.

Amelia's father, though burdened by the weight of his actions, found a semblance of peace in the aftermath. He knew that his decision to take matters into his own hands had been born of desperation and love. As he watched his daughter begin to heal, he understood that sometimes, the only way to combat darkness was to shine an unrelenting light upon it, no matter the cost.

And so, life in Thornfield resumed, forever marked by the shadows of the past but strengthened by the unwavering resolve of its people. The town had faced its greatest nightmare and had emerged, scarred but victorious. The Boogeyman was no more, and in his absence, the residents of Thornfield began to find hope once again, rebuilding their lives on the foundations of resilience and unity.

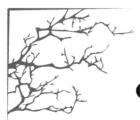

Chapter Sixteen

IN THE EERIE SILENCE that followed the crackling of flames and the wailing sirens, the volunteer fire department stood in their disheveled pajamas, their breaths visible in the cold night air. Their weary eyes fixated upon the charred remnants of what was once a cozy home. But it wasn't the scorched ruins that sent chills down their spines—it was the haunting presence of the body they stumbled upon amidst the ashes.

A man lay there, motionless and seemingly lifeless. But as their curiosity demanded closer inspection, they found the faint, erratic rise and fall of his chest, like the labored breaths of a creature on the brink of oblivion. They wasted no time, scooping him up with utmost care and hustling him into the waiting ambulance, its red and blue lights casting eerie shadows across the devastated neighborhood.

The journey to the emergency room echoed with the piercing wails of the siren, blending seamlessly with the manic beats racing through their hearts. The man's condition was precarious, teetering on the precipice of life and death. The ambulance navigated the winding roads with a desperate urgency, swerving around dark corners as if pursued by unseen forces.

Once at the hospital, the team of surgeons sprang into action like a well-oiled machine, their hands moving as if guided by something beyond mere human skill. The clock ticked away, mercilessly edging towards a sinister future. For sixteen long hours, they toiled relentlessly under the sterile lights, their focus a testament to their collective will to salvage what remained of a battered soul.

Time seemed to stretch, unraveling like a twisted thread, as the surgeons fought against the encroaching darkness. Twice, the man flatlined on the operating table, his lifeline hanging by the slenderest of threads. They battled against his imminent demise, willing life back into his shattered body with every ounce of strength they had left.

Against all odds, the Boogeyman of Thornfield showed a resilience that defied comprehension. He emerged from the abyss, gasping for air as if he had slipped through the clutches of the Grim Reaper himself. Survival coursed through his veins, a testament to the indomitable spirit that refuses to yield in the face of horror.

As news of his miraculous survival trickled through the hospital corridors, whispers filled the air. Superstitions whispered in hushed tones, suggesting that something sinister had granted him a second chance at life. The Boogeyman, now forever marked by the hands of justice, had become a legend—a living, breathing nightmare that refused to be extinguished.

The doctors and nurses, seasoned professionals who had witnessed countless medical miracles, were shaken by the man's sheer will to live. They whispered among themselves, sharing uneasy glances as they recounted the harrowing hours spent fighting for his life. Some speculated that he was no ordinary man, that he was fueled by an unholy force that defied the natural order.

As the Boogeyman lay in his hospital bed, recovering from the brink of death, the small town of Thornfield buzzed with fear and curiosity. The news of his survival spread like wildfire, igniting old fears and stirring up memories best left forgotten. Parents clutched their children tighter, and doors were bolted shut with renewed vigilance. The nightmare that had haunted their lives was not over; it had merely taken on a new, more insidious form.

Amelia's father, who had been among those who sought vigilante justice, felt a cold dread settle in his bones when he heard the news. The man who had tormented his daughter, who had invaded their lives with his monstrous presence, was still alive. The sense of closure he had desperately sought now felt like a cruel illusion. The specter of the Boogeyman loomed larger than ever, casting a shadow over the fragile peace they had fought so hard to reclaim.

The townspeople, though terrified, were also curious. They wanted to see the man who had defied death, to glimpse the monster who had become the stuff of legends. Crowds gathered outside the hospital, a macabre fascination drawing them to the place where the Boogeyman clung to life. The media descended upon Thornfield, eager to capture the story of a town gripped by fear and a man who seemed to embody evil itself.

Inside the hospital, security was tightened. The authorities were acutely aware of the public's unrest and the potential for violence. They stationed guards outside the Boogeyman's room, a constant reminder of the threat he posed even in his weakened state. The doctors continued their work, but the atmosphere was charged with tension and unease.

Amelia's father, consumed by his own torment, visited the hospital one night, slipping past the guards with the ease born of desperation. He stood outside the room, staring at the figure lying in the bed, tubes and machines keeping him tethered to life. The urge to finish what they had started, to end the nightmare once and for all, surged within him. But as he watched the rise and fall of the man's chest, he felt a conflict tearing at his soul.

He was a protector, a father driven by love and a fierce need to safeguard his family. Yet, the act of taking a life, even one as twisted as the Boogeyman's, weighed heavily on him. He remembered the violence, the blood, and the fire. He remembered the look in his daughter's eyes, the pain that no amount of vengeance could erase. With a heavy heart, he turned away, leaving the Boogeyman to whatever fate awaited him.

As days turned into weeks, the Boogeyman's condition stabilized. The doctors, despite their own misgivings, were committed to saving him. They patched up his broken body, but the scars of his actions, both physical and psychological, remained. The man who had once instilled fear in the hearts of Thornfield now lay helpless, a ghost of his former self.

Yet, the question lingered: what would become of him? The justice system would take its course, but for the people of Thornfield, no sentence could truly erase the horror they had endured. The Boogeyman had become a symbol, a dark reminder of the evil that can lurk within the human soul. His survival was a paradox, a testament to the fragility of life and the endurance of fear.

In the end, the Boogeyman's fate was sealed not just by the courts, but by the collective will of a community determined to move forward. Thornfield, though scarred, found strength in its unity. The nightmare that had once gripped them loosened its hold, replaced by a steely resolve to protect one another and heal together.

For Amelia's father, the journey was far from over. The road to healing was long and fraught with challenges, but he walked it with the knowledge that he had faced the darkness and survived. He had not succumbed to the same evil that had threatened his family. Instead, he chose to channel his pain into rebuilding, to create a future where his daughter could once again find peace.

Thornfield, too, began to heal. The fires that had consumed the Boogeyman's lair became a symbol of renewal. Out of the ashes, a new community spirit emerged, stronger and more resilient than before. They had faced their greatest fear and, together, they had overcome it.

As the Boogeyman lay in his hospital bed, a new chapter in Thornfield's history began. It was a story not just of survival, but of hope and redemption. The shadows that had once loomed so large now receded, replaced by the light of a community united in its determination to protect its own.

And so, the nightmare that refused to die became a part of Thornfield's past, a lesson etched into their collective memory. The Boogeyman had not won. The people of Thornfield, with their indomitable spirit and unwavering resolve, had triumphed over the darkness, forging a path towards a brighter, safer future.

Chapter Seventeen

IN THE AFTERMATH OF tragedy, the whispers of the macabre are seldom far behind. For there are corners of our realm, hidden in the deepest recesses of our minds, where darkness thrives. The true nature of the Boogeyman, waiting patiently for the perfect moment to seize his prey once more. The Boogeyman never dies.

Months passed, and Amelia's once feeble grip on reality began to strengthen. The doctors tirelessly probed her mind, dissecting the deepest recesses of her traumatic memories. In the padded walls of their safe haven, she found solace and redemption. With each session, the Boogeyman's taunting whispers grew fainter, the shackles around her soul loosening ever so slightly.

Finally, the day arrived when Amelia was deemed fit to be released from her captivity once more. Her parents, cautious yet hopeful, welcomed her back into their arms. The air in their house crackled with anxiety, as each step Amelia took threatened to unravel the fragile tapestry they had so painstakingly woven. They held their breath, praying that this time, the nightmare was truly over.

For a while, it seemed as though harmony had been restored. Amelia dutifully took her medicine, a daily vow of self-preservation. But her parents knew the truth; the beast that dwelled within her was far from vanquished. They watched her fragile composure, the way her eyes darted around the room, forever searching for shadows that were no longer there.

And so, the cycle continued. The Boogeyman haunted Amelia's dreams, lingering in the corners of her perception. Through the haze of her medicated state, she fought a battle against the tide of her own mind. The darkness clawed at the edges of her sanity, threatening to pull her under once more.

Every day, Amelia found herself engaged in a harrowing battle, but it was not against a tangible foe or external threat. No, her struggle was one waged within the treacherous depths of her own mind. The trauma she had endured had become a constant companion, an insidious haunt that whispered malevolently in her ear, the sinister Boogeyman lurking just beyond the realm of perception.

His scratchy voice, a hollow echo, would make promises of torture and despair, reminding her that the concept of safety was nothing but a fragile illusion. It reveled in her vulnerability, feeding off the fear that coursed through her veins like a poison. No matter how hard she fought to silence its malicious discourse, the Boogeyman persisted, relentless in its torment.

Amelia's days were spent teetering on the precipice of sanity, her once vibrant spirit overshadowed by an impenetrable darkness. The world, once filled with colors and laughter, had become a muddled canvas of gray and muted tones. Joy seemed but a distant memory, a dream lost in the haze of her tortured reality.

She would close her eyes, seeking solace in the sanctuary of her mind, only to find it occupied by the harbingers of her deepest fears. Nightmares became her nocturnal companions, their vivid imagery seeping into her waking hours, blurring the line between what was real and what lived solely in the realm of nightmares.

Sleep had become a treacherous minefield, a vicious battleground between her mind and the haunting terrors that lay within. In the depths of her subconscious, dreams wrestled with reality, intermingling until she could no longer discern one from the other. The line between sleep and nightmare had blurred, trapping Amelia in a torment she could not escape.

Every night, as darkness fell and the world around her succumbed to slumber, Amelia would brace herself for the onslaught of terror that awaited her. The Boogeyman, ever watchful, would creep into her dreams, turning them into nightmarish landscapes where safety was an illusion and hope was a distant memory. She would wake in a cold sweat, her heart racing, the shadows of her dreams clinging to her like a second skin.

Her parents, though supportive, were helpless in the face of her nightly battles. They watched, hearts breaking, as their daughter struggled against an unseen enemy. They whispered words of comfort, held her through the worst of it, but they could not shield her from the horrors that lurked in her mind. Their love was a beacon, but even it could not pierce the darkness that enveloped her.

Amelia's doctors adjusted her medication, seeking the right balance to keep the nightmares at bay without numbing her entirely. Therapy sessions continued, each one a painful excavation of the trauma she had endured. Progress was slow, marked by small victories and crushing setbacks. But through it all, Amelia fought on, her spirit battered but unbroken.

She found small moments of peace in the mundane routines of daily life. The simple act of watering the garden, the rhythmic strokes of a paintbrush on canvas, the warmth of her mother's embrace—all these things grounded her, reminded her that there was more to life than the shadows that haunted her. She clung to these moments, drawing strength from them as she navigated the treacherous path of recovery.

Yet, even in her most peaceful moments, the Boogeyman was never far away. He lurked in the periphery, a constant reminder of the darkness that could consume her at any moment. Amelia knew she could never let her guard down, that vigilance was her only defense against the horrors that threatened to engulf her.

One day, as the sun dipped below the horizon, casting long shadows across the yard, Amelia sat on the porch, her sketchbook in hand. She had taken up drawing as a way to channel her fears, to give form to the formless terrors that plagued her. Her sketches were dark, filled with twisted figures and shadowy landscapes, but they were also a testament to her resilience.

As she drew, she felt a presence behind her. She turned, half expecting to see the Boogeyman standing there, his eyes gleaming with disgusting glee. But it was only her father, his face lined with worry and love. He sat beside her, watching as she sketched, offering silent support.

They sat together in the fading light, a father and daughter united in their struggle against an unseen enemy. In that moment, Amelia felt a glimmer of hope. She was not alone in her battle. She had her family, her doctors, her own indomitable spirit. The Boogeyman might never die, but neither would she.

She would continue to fight, to seek out the light in the darkest of places. The road ahead was long and fraught with challenges, but she was determined to walk it, one step at a time. She would reclaim her life, piece by piece, until the Boogeyman was nothing more than a distant memory, a shadow that could no longer harm her.

In the end, Amelia's story was not just one of survival, but of courage and resilience. She faced the darkness head-on, refusing to let it define her. She chose to live, to find joy in the small moments, to build a future free from the grip of fear. And in doing so, she proved that even in the face of unimaginable horror, the human spirit was unbreakable.

As the days turned into weeks and then months, Amelia continued to fight her silent battle. The Boogeyman remained a lurking presence, but his hold on her had weakened. She found strength in her family, in the routines of daily life, in the small victories that marked her progress. She learned to live with the shadows, to face her fears with courage and determination.

Her parents, ever watchful, drew hope from her resilience. They saw their daughter reclaiming her life, step by step, and they dared to believe that the nightmare was finally fading. Thornfield, too, began to heal. The community, scarred but unbroken, came together in a spirit of unity and support. They had faced their darkest fears and emerged stronger for it.

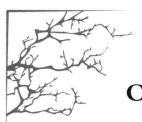

Chapter Eighteen

AMELIA SAT ON THE EDGE of her bed, the soft glow of the setting sun casting a warm, golden hue across her room. She glanced around at the familiar surroundings, the walls adorned with sketches and paintings that bore the marks of her struggles and triumphs. Each piece was a testament to her resilience, yet they also served as a constant reminder of the darkness she could never fully escape.

As she brushed her hair, now long and cascading in soft waves around her shoulders, she couldn't help but feel the weight of the years pressing down on her. She had grown into a young woman, her beauty blossoming despite the shadows that lingered in her eyes. But her reflection in the mirror revealed more than just physical transformation; it mirrored the scars etched deep within her soul.

Her mind wandered back to her childhood, a time that should have been filled with innocence and joy. Instead, it had been marred by fear and pain, the Boogeyman casting a long, dark shadow over her formative years. She remembered the nights spent clutching her pillow, trembling in terror as she awaited the next nightmare. The days were no better, her mind a battleground of dread and anxiety.

Why me? She often thought. Tears welled in her eyes, blurring her vision as she looked out the window at the darkening sky. What did she do to live a life like this?

The questions had haunted her for as long as she could remember. She had spent countless hours in therapy, digging through the layers of her trauma, seeking answers that never came. The doctors had given her coping mechanisms, medications to dull the edges of her fear, but nothing could erase the memories that clung to her like a second skin.

Amelia's heart ached with a profound weariness. She was tired of living a life dictated by fear, tired of the constant battle against an enemy that lurked within her own mind. She longed for a sense of normalcy, for a life unburdened by the weight of her past. She yearned to be like other girls her age, carefree and confident, basking in the glow of their youth.

But her confidence was shattered, a fragile construct that crumbled under the slightest pressure. She avoided social gatherings, fearful of the whispers and the sideways glances. She felt like an outsider, perpetually on the fringes of a world she could never fully join. Her beauty, once a source of pride, now felt like a cruel irony, highlighting the chasm between her appearance and her internal turmoil.

In the quiet moments, when she was alone with her thoughts, Amelia often found herself questioning her worth. She was the victim, yet she carried the guilt of a culprit. She felt as though she had somehow invited the darkness into her life, as if her very existence was a beacon for the Boogeyman's existence. The weight of this misplaced guilt was crushing, sapping her strength and dimming her spirit.

She looked up at the sky, the first stars beginning to twinkle against the deepening blue. When will it end? She would ask the sky, her voice breaking with emotion. When will the day arrive when she could feel finally free?

The tears spilled over, tracing a path down her cheeks. She felt a profound sense of injustice, a bitterness that gnawed at her heart. She had done nothing to deserve this fate, yet she was the one left to pick up the pieces, to navigate a world that seemed intent on reminding her of her fragility. The Boogeyman might never die, but his presence in her life had taken something irreplaceable from her—her sense of self, her confidence, her joy.

As she sat there, Amelia felt a flicker of defiance ignite within her. It was a small flame, easily extinguished, but it was there nonetheless. She had survived this long, had faced the darkness and come out the other side. She might be weary, but she was not broken. Not yet.

She thought, maybe one day she'll find her way out of this. The path ahead was uncertain, the shadows ever-present, but Amelia knew she had to keep moving forward. She had to believe that there was a future where the nightmares no longer held sway, where she could live a life free from the fear that had defined her for so long. It was a fragile hope, but it was hers, and she clung to it with all the strength she could muster.

As the night deepened, Amelia wiped away her tears and took a deep breath. She had faced the Boogeyman and survived. She could face whatever came next. The journey was far from over, but she was still standing, still fighting. And maybe, just maybe, that was enough.

She closed her eyes, allowing the darkness to envelop her, but this time she did not shy away. She faced it head-on, a silent vow forming in her heart. She would reclaim her life, piece by piece, until the shadows that haunted her were nothing more than a distant memory. And in that reclamation, she would find her strength, her confidence, her joy. For now, though, she allowed herself to rest. She had earned it, after all.

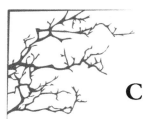

Chapter Nineteen

THE NIGHTS WERE AMELIA'S greatest torment, each one a relentless cycle of terror and exhaustion. Her bed, meant to be a sanctuary, had become a battlefield where she fought for a semblance of peace. The room, once a refuge adorned with comforting mementos, now felt like a cage where shadows danced and whispered, their forms morphing into the sinister outline of the Boogeyman.

Night after night, Amelia's sleep was drenched in sweat, her body a mere vessel for her tortured psyche. The ethereal whispers of sleep's descent would be abruptly shattered by the icy breath of the Boogeyman. In the cloak of darkness, he would slither into her dreams, his presence unmistakable, and his grip relentless. The nightmares were not just figments of her imagination; they were vivid, visceral experiences that left her gasping for air, heart pounding against her chest as if seeking refuge in the safety of wakefulness.

With every startled awakening, Amelia would lie in the darkness, her pulse racing, the remnants of her dreams clinging to her consciousness like cobwebs. The torment followed her like a shadow. It clung to her thoughts, latching onto her every waking moment, refusing to loosen its grip even as daylight breached the horizon. Morning light brought no solace, only a brief respite before the cycle began anew.

The claws of her PTSD dug deep into her fragile reality, sinking their talons into every fiber of her being. Its tendrils reached out, snaking their way into her mind, leaving her trembling and defenseless to the horrors that lurked in the depths. It was a constant battle, fought not on distant fields but in the very core of her existence. Her mind was a labyrinth, each corner hiding the specter of her past, each turn a potential encounter with the Boogeyman.

Amelia longed for respite, for a chance to break free from the clutches of her fractured mind. But the nightmares persisted, ruthless in their pursuit. The Boogeyman reveled in her pain, relishing in the fear he instilled, savoring the taste of her anguish. He knew no mercy, no compassion, only the insidious desire to keep her captive within the labyrinth of her own torment. His voice, a hollow echo of malevolence, promised unending terror and despair.

She remembered nights spent huddled under the covers, as a child believing that the thin fabric could protect her from the horrors lurking in the dark. Those nights seemed like a distant memory, yet the fear felt just as real, just as potent. The Boogeyman's hold over her was unyielding, a testament to the profound impact of her trauma. The safety she sought was elusive, a mirage that disappeared the moment she reached for it.

Amelia knew that she was no longer the same person. The trauma had crystallized within her, forming an indelible mark that served as a constant reminder of what she had endured. She had become a living testament to the power of pain, its tendrils reaching into every aspect of her being, gnawing away at her very essence. Her laughter was now rare, a hollow echo of the joy she once knew. The vibrant colors of her world had dulled, replaced by shades of gray that mirrored her inner turmoil.

She often found herself standing at the window, staring at the night sky, searching for answers in the vast expanse above. The stars, once a source of wonder, now seemed indifferent to her suffering. The universe continued its ceaseless march, oblivious to the pain of a single soul. Amelia's heart ached with the weight of her loneliness, a profound sense of isolation that stemmed from feeling perpetually misunderstood.

For deep within her soul, she believed that one day the flicker of hope would be extinguished, that she would embrace the darkness as the ghosts of her trauma claimed their residency. Amelia knew that even amidst the darkest of nights, the dawn would eventually break and with it, her mind, as had her innocence not that long ago. The Boogeyman's whispers might linger, but she fought his sinister grip with every ounce of strength she could muster. Yet, that strength was waning, each battle leaving her more drained than the last.

Her life had become a series of endless struggles, her future uncertain. She wondered if she would ever find peace, if the nightmares would ever cease. The hope she clung to felt like a fragile thread, stretched thin by the weight of her despair. Amelia's spirit, once bright and unyielding, now flickered like a candle in the wind, its flame threatened by the relentless storm of her memories.

As she stood at the window, the first light of dawn breaking on the horizon, she felt a deep, abiding hopelessness. The new day brought no promise of respite, only the continuation of her struggle. The Boogeyman's shadow loomed over her, a constant reminder of the horrors that had shaped her life. Amelia's heart ached with the knowledge that the end of her torment was nowhere in sight, and the path to a normal life seemed forever out of reach.

Her tears flowed freely, a silent testament to her suffering. She felt a profound sense of injustice, a bitterness that gnawed at her soul. She had done nothing to deserve this fate, yet she was the one left to pick up the pieces, to navigate a world that seemed intent on reminding her of her fragility. The Boogeyman might never die, but his presence in her life had taken something irreplaceable from her—her sense of self, her confidence, her joy.

Amelia closed her eyes, allowing the darkness to envelop her. There was no light, no hope. Only the night, endless and unyielding, and the silent, unspoken question that haunted her every waking moment: when will she be free?

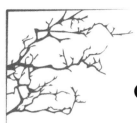

Chapter Twenty

HE LAY THERE, EYES closed, an enigma wrapped in bandages, suspended between life and oblivion. Outside the sterile walls of his hospital room, the world moved on, the humdrum of daily life uninterrupted. People hurried through the holiday season, unaware of the slumbering beast lurking amongst them. Thornfield, a town seemingly peaceful and quaint, held its secrets tightly, and the monster was one of them—a dark chapter in its otherwise idyllic narrative.

Time had passed like sand trickling through the fingers of a forgotten god. The monster's mind danced in a constantly shifting haze of memories and dreams, blending into a kaleidoscope of pain and suffering. Visions of fire and shadow intertwined, a nightmarish ballet of anguish. But deep within the chaos, a flicker of consciousness remained, an ember waiting to be reignited.

On that icy Christmas morning, as families gathered around trees adorned with flickering lights, exchanging gifts and basking in the warmth of togetherness, the monster stirred. The hospital staff bustled about, immersed in their routines, unaware of the storm brewing in their midst. The air grew tense, as if a shard of lightning had sliced through the tranquil atmosphere.

Slowly, like a specter awakening from an eternal slumber, the monster's eyes fluttered open. Glimmers of light danced amidst the darkness of his sight, and he beheld a world reborn. The memories, the pain, all returned in a deafening roar, but beneath it all, there was a newfound clarity, an unearthly determination clawing its way to the surface. He had survived the fire that had sought to consume him, emerging from the inferno not as a victim, but as a harbinger of retribution.

The monster, now awake, blended seamlessly into the backdrop of Thornfield's bustling hospital. He became a phantom haunting the corridors, hidden among the shadows of its sterile walls. The whispers of nurses permeated the air, speculating the extent of his injuries, unknowing of the true horror they spoke of. His burned flesh, gradually healing, left behind grotesque scars, a twisted map of his torment. Each day, as his physical wounds closed, his resolve grew stronger.

And as his strength returned, so too did memories of the fateful night that had brought him to this abyss. The fire that tore through his life, consuming everything in its path. His screams that echoed like a symphony in his ears, blending with the howling wind outside. Thornfield had forgotten him, cast him aside, assuming he would forever rest in the asylum of oblivion. But they were wrong. The monster was not willing to embrace the darkness just yet.

He yearned for justice, for revenge against the town that had condemned him to this purgatory and made him define his existence in pain. With every step, he planned his vengeance meticulously, weaving a web of terror that would ensnare all those who had wronged him. His mind was a cauldron of dark fantasies, each thought a venomous thread in the tapestry of his revenge.

The memories of that fateful night replayed in his mind, vivid and relentless. The crackling of flames, the acrid smell of smoke, the searing pain as the fire licked at his skin. He could still hear the screams—his own and those of his family—echoing in the inferno. The fire had not just consumed his home; it had devoured his very soul, leaving behind a husk of a man, transformed into something monstrous by the crucible of his suffering.

He remembered the faces of those who had wronged him, the ones who had turned their backs in his hour of need. They had condemned him, judged him without a second thought. The betrayal had cut deeper than any physical wound, festering within him like a cancer. Their faces were etched into his memory, each one a target for the vengeance that now fueled his every thought.

On that fateful Christmas morning, as the snow fell gracefully, nature naively celebrating the season of joy and peace, the Boogeyman of Thornfield moved with a newfound purpose. He was like a chess master about to unleash a game-changing gambit, every move calculated, every step deliberate. The darkness that fueled his being had transformed him, forged a monster out of ashes and embers. No longer human, he had become an agent of chaos, his retribution a symphony he would conduct with unmatched precision.

He wandered the hospital halls, a shadow among the living, absorbing every detail, every weakness. The town of Thornfield had forgotten, but soon, they would remember every sin and every transgression. They would embrace the fear that had eluded them for so long, the fear that he would orchestrate with the same care that a maestro brings to a grand composition.

As he moved through the hospital, his mind crafted his plans with meticulous detail. He imagined the looks of terror, the pleas for mercy. He envisioned the chaos he would unleash upon Thornfield, a storm of retribution that would leave no stone unturned. Each scar on his body was a reminder, a mark of his rebirth. The Boogeyman of Thornfield was awake, and the nightmare had only just begun.

In the dark recesses of his mind, he replayed the scenes of his suffering, each memory fueling his resolve. He saw the faces of his betrayers, their expressions twisted in fear and guilt. He heard their voices, pleading for forgiveness, begging for a mercy they had denied him. His heart, if it could still be called that, beat with a cold, relentless rhythm, each thud a promise of the vengeance to come.

The monster's journey was one of both physical and psychological torment. Each step he took was a testament to his transformation, a journey from victim to villain. His once human heart had become a furnace of hatred, each beat echoing with the cries of the innocent and the damned. The fire that had sought to destroy him had only forged him anew, stronger and more determined than ever.

The corridors of the hospital, once places of healing and hope, now seemed to echo with his presence. The sterile white walls, the hum of machinery, the soft murmurs of the staff—all became the backdrop for his dark symphony. He was a ghost among the living, unseen and unnoticed, yet ever-present. The Boogeyman had returned, and his vengeance would be swift and merciless.

Each night, as the world slept, he planned his retribution. The faces of those who had wronged him haunted his dreams, their cries for mercy a lullaby to his vengeful soul. He would visit them, one by one, and they would know the true meaning of fear. Thornfield would remember the monster it had created, the darkness it had unleashed.

And as the snow continued to fall outside, blanketing the world in a deceptive purity, the Boogeyman of Thornfield prepared to unleash his wrath. The town, blissfully unaware, continued to celebrate the season of joy and peace. But beneath the surface, the storm was brewing, a tempest of vengeance that would soon engulf them all.

The monster's scars, both physical and emotional, were a testament to his transformation. Each one told a story, a chapter in the dark saga of his life. The pain he had endured had not broken him; it had remade him, forged him into a creature of relentless determination. He was no longer a victim, but a harbinger of retribution.

In the quiet moments, when the hospital was still and the world outside was hushed by the falling snow, he would look at his reflection. The bandages had come off, revealing the twisted, scarred visage beneath. His eyes, once filled with warmth and humanity, now burned with a cold, unyielding fire. The Boogeyman stared back at him, a reflection of his inner darkness, a reminder of the path he had chosen.

He knew he was not a very good man but he thought he didn't deserve the torment he went through. His journey from victim to villain was complete. He had embraced the darkness within, allowing it to guide him. The pain and suffering he had endured had not broken him; they had forged him into something more. He was the Boogeyman of Thornfield, a creature of nightmare, a specter of vengeance.

The monster's mind, once a battleground of memories and dreams, was now a weapon of precise calculation. Every thought, every plan was a step towards his ultimate goal. Thornfield would pay for its sins, and he would be the instrument of its retribution. The Boogeyman had awoken, and the nightmare had only just begun.

Chapter Twenty-One

IN THE HUSHED SILENCE of their home, Amelia's father sat glued to the television, awaiting the nightly news report. The air around him was thick with tension, almost tangible, as if it had taken physical form and wrapped itself around the family. Every tick of the clock echoed like a heartbeat, a relentless reminder of the weight they carried. Dread clung to their every breath, a manifestation of the guilt lurking within them. They knew that the early morning hours had brought news of a fire, a house consumed by violent flames, and the discovery of an unidentifiable body. But it was only now, in the afterglow of their clandestine act, that the true weight of their actions began to settle upon their hearts.

Days turned into weeks, and still, they watched eagerly for any shred of information that would satisfy their gnawing curiosity. The television became their oracle, each broadcast a potential harbinger of their fate. They craved closure, a resolution to the twisted puzzle they had unknowingly become a part of. But the news remained silent, cruelly withholding the identity of the unrecognizable corpse. The unanswered questions hung in the air, suffocating them with their weight.

Relief whispered ever so faintly in their veins. Relief that they had successfully carried out their vigilante justice in the dead of night. They had rid the world of someone they deemed deserving of punishment, someone who had slipped through the porcelain cracks of the justice system. But even amidst the relief, fear clawed its way up their spines like the bony fingers of the Boogeyman that still lurked in their shadows. The Boogeyman—an insidious force that always seemed to be lurking, invisible to prying eyes. They had hoped that by taking matters into their own trembling hands, they would be able to banish the evil for good. But the unidentifiable nature of the body, the absence of a name or a face, left them vulnerable to doubts and fears that crept relentlessly through the night.

Amelia, their innocent daughter, sensed the unease that cast its pall over their household. She saw the flickering unease in her parents' eyes, the way their voices quivered ever so slightly. And yet, she remained oblivious to the true nature of their secret. She yearned for answers, for a sense of closure that seemed forever beyond her grasp. She was a sensitive barometer to the emotional weather in their home, detecting the storm that brewed beneath the surface even if she couldn't understand its origins.

The worst part of it all was that Amelia knew that the Boogeyman still roamed freely in the darkness of her mind. Unidentified, uncaught, and perhaps forever elusive. No matter how much she willed it, closure would forever evade her. The uncertainty gnawed at her soul, like a sinister beast slowly consuming her innocence. Night after night, she found herself drenched in sweat, her body a mere vessel for her tortured psyche. The Boogeyman, ever-present in her nightmares, slithered into her dreams, his presence unmistakable, and his grip relentless.

Each morning, Amelia would wake with a start, heart pounding against her chest as if seeking refuge in the safety of wakefulness. But the torment followed her like a shadow. It clung to her thoughts, latching onto her every waking moment, refusing to loosen its grip even as daylight breached the horizon. Her once vibrant dreams were now plagued by a relentless darkness, a stark contrast to the innocent reveries of her childhood.

Amelia's father, with guilt as his constant companion, replayed the night of the fire in his mind. The match, the accelerant, the towering inferno that swallowed the house whole. He had watched it burn, a grim satisfaction mixed with a deep, gnawing regret. They had taken a life, or so they believed, yet the silence from the authorities tormented them. Who was the body in the house? Had they truly rid the world of a monster, or had they made a terrible mistake?

Her mother, though outwardly composed, was a storm of emotions beneath the surface. Each day, she went through the motions, a mask of normalcy hiding her inner turmoil. She cleaned the house, cooked meals, and tended to her garden, but her thoughts were always elsewhere, tangled in the web of what they had done. The garden, once a place of solace, now felt like a graveyard, each plant a reminder of the life they had extinguished. She planted new seeds, hoping to bring forth new life, but the weight of their secret tainted everything she touched.

Her father threw himself into his work, trying to escape the torment of his thoughts. He stayed late at the office, avoiding the accusatory silence of their home. The walls, once comforting, now felt like a prison, each room a cell where his guilt festered. He took up running, pounding the pavement in a futile attempt to outrun his conscience. But no matter how fast or how far he ran, the darkness followed, an inescapable shadow.

The town of Thornfield continued on, blissfully unaware of the storm brewing within the walls of Amelia's home. Neighbors exchanged pleasantries, oblivious to the secrets that lay hidden beneath the surface. Life went on, unchanged, as if the fire and the mysterious body were nothing more than a distant memory. But for Amelia and her family, the nightmare was far from over.

Spring arrived, bringing with it the promise of renewal, but for Amelia's family, the change of seasons offered no reprieve. The garden bloomed, the trees budded with new leaves, yet the darkness within their home remained. Each day was a struggle, a battle against the guilt and fear that had taken root in their hearts.

Amelia's parents, once so sure of their actions, now questioned everything. Had they truly rid the world of a monster, or had they committed an unforgivable sin? The questions gnawed at them, a constant reminder of the price they had paid for their vigilante justice. They had hoped for closure, for a resolution to the twisted puzzle they had become a part of, but the silence from the authorities was a cruel and unrelenting torment.

Amelia, sensing the growing tension, withdrew further into herself. She spent hours in her room, lost in books and music, trying to escape the oppressive atmosphere of their home. But no matter how hard she tried, the darkness followed her, a constant companion. She dreamed of a life free from fear, free from the shadows that had taken hold of her family, but those dreams felt as distant and unreachable as the stars.

The worst part of it all was the uncertainty. Amelia knew that the Boogeyman still roamed freely in the darkness—unidentified, uncaught, and perhaps forever elusive. The uncertainty gnawed at her soul, like a sinister beast slowly consuming her innocence. She longed for answers, for a sense of closure, but it seemed forever beyond her grasp.

And so, Amelia's family carried on, haunted by their deeds and tormented by the unknown. Secrets held tightly within their hearts, gnarled and distorted, forever altering the fabric of their once ordinary lives. They found no solace, their fate forever entwined with the shadows they had unleashed. As the days turned into months, the weight of their secret grew heavier, a burden they would carry with them always.

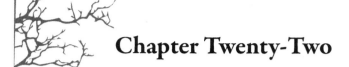

Chapter Twenty-Two

CHRISTMAS WAS NOT THE morning the Boogeyman had anticipated waking up. It had been three long years since his eyes had last caressed the dim light of reality, and now, here he was, thrust back into the cruel grasp of consciousness. The sterile white of the hospital room, the beeping of machines, the sensation of tubes snaking into his veins—it all felt alien, as if he had been reborn into a nightmare.

The medical staff buzzed around him, resembling a hive of white-coated bees in his groggy state. They poked and prodded, inserting tubes and wires into his fragile body with an unsettling detachment. Their faces were masks of professionalism, betraying no emotion as they examined the physical remnants of a man who had become legend. His numb mind struggled to process this sudden influx of activity, desperately seeking some semblance of understanding as to why they had revived him. Every jab of a needle and every beep of the monitor felt like an intrusion into the limbo where he had resided for so long.

Eventually, the tests concluded, and the room fell eerily silent. The discomforting absence of sound was a stark contrast to the chaotic symphony that had enveloped him just moments before. This silence, however, was heavy with unspoken questions and unvoiced fears. Shadows crept in at the edges of his vision, darkening his already troubled mind, casting elongated figures that danced mockingly on the walls.

The door creaked open, incapable of obscuring the detective's presence. The mere sight of the man in the rumpled trench coat sent shivers down the Boogeyman's spine. There was an air of certainty about him, as if he already knew the terrifying truth that lay buried within the Boogeyman's fractured memories. The detective's eyes, sharp and unyielding, bore into him, dissecting his very soul.

They sat facing each other, the detective's gaze piercing through the Boogeyman with an unyielding intensity. Words danced on the tip of the detective's tongue, threatening to spill forth and shatter the remaining fragments of the Boogeyman's fragile sanity. The silence between them was a taut string, ready to snap at the slightest provocation.

Monsters are real and ghosts are real, too. They live inside us and sometimes, they win. The name rolled off the detective's tongue like a dark incantation, conjuring memories that the Boogeyman had so desperately tried to bury. The statement was not just an observation, but a pronouncement, a grim reminder of the horrors that lay within.

The Boogeyman could only manage a feeble nod, his throat constricted by the nightmare that had unraveled in that godforsaken place. Dark corners whispered secrets to him, twisted whispers that echoed through the halls of his mind even now. His consciousness was a battleground, memories clawing their way to the surface, each one a fragment of his broken psyche.

The room seemed to spin as images blurred before the Boogeyman's eyes, jumbled fragments of a horrifying tableau. Bleeding walls, chilling laughter, and the sulfurous scent of evil permeated every inch of Thornfield. He documented it all, desperate to capture the essence of terror that thrived within those walls, only to become the very subject of his own macabre narrative. The memories were like shards of glass, each one cutting into his soul, each one a reminder of the darkness he could never escape.

News of the Boogeyman's resurrection spread like wildfire, plastered across screens and newspapers alike. The world marveled at the fact that he was still alive, released from the clutches of the hospital that had become his prison. His name, once whispered in fear, now echoed with a newfound trepidation. The legend of the Boogeyman had been reignited, and with it, the fear that had once gripped the town of Thornfield.

As the Boogeyman stepped into the unforgiving embrace of the outside world, his heart churned with a mix of dread and anticipation. The world had moved on without him, yet his presence would forever stain it. He knew that he could never truly escape his own legacy, that a darkness would forever reside within him, lurking in the corners of his mind. The air outside was cold, biting, a stark contrast to the sterile warmth of the hospital room. It was a cruel reminder that the world was indifferent to his suffering.

The boogeyman had awakened, his presence once again staining the world. And although his motives remained cloaked in shadows, the detective knew that the whispers of Thornfield still lingered, haunting every step the Boogeyman took. The detective, too, felt the weight of the Boogeyman's return, an unspoken challenge that hung between them. The hunter and the hunted, their fates intertwined in a dance as old as time.

The streets of Thornfield were unchanged, yet everything felt different to the Boogeyman. He walked through the town like a ghost, unseen but ever-present. Each corner, each alleyway held memories of his past, echoes of his deeds. The townsfolk went about their lives, blissfully unaware of the storm that had been unleashed. But the Boogeyman knew that it was only a matter of time before they felt his presence.

He wandered through the town, absorbing the sights and sounds, each one a reminder of the world he had left behind. The laughter of children, the chatter of neighbors, the everyday bustle of life—it all felt like an alien landscape to him now. He was an intruder in a world that had moved on, a relic of a past that refused to die.

In the dead of night, he found himself drawn to the old ruins of Thornfield Manor, the place where his transformation had begun. The once grand estate was now a decaying husk, a fitting monument to his fractured soul. He stood before the ruins, memories flooding his mind, each one a dagger to his heart. The fire, the screams, the overwhelming sense of loss—it all came rushing back, a tidal wave of pain and regret.

The Boogeyman knew that he could never escape his past, that the darkness within him would always find a way to the surface. But he also knew that he could not simply succumb to it. There was a part of him that still yearned for redemption, a sliver of humanity that refused to be extinguished. As he stood before the ruins of Thornfield Manor, he made a silent vow—to confront his demons, to seek out those who had wronged him, and to find some semblance of peace.

The detective, ever vigilant, knew that the Boogeyman's return was only the beginning. He had seen the darkness in the man's eyes, the unrelenting hunger for vengeance. But he also saw something else—a glimmer of hope, a chance for redemption. The detective resolved to keep a close watch on the Boogeyman, to be there when the final reckoning came.

For now, the Boogeyman walked the streets of Thornfield, a phantom of his former self. But within him burned a fire, a determination to reclaim his humanity. The journey ahead would be long and arduous, fraught with danger and temptation. But the Boogeyman was ready. The nightmare had only just begun, and he would face it head-on, no longer a slave to his fears but a warrior in the battle for his soul.

Chapter Twenty-Three

AMELIA AWOKE WITH A start, her heart pounding against her chest like a prisoner desperate to break free. The room spun around her, tilting and swirling like a morbid carousel. The taste of bile lingered in her mouth, the sour remnants of her distress staining her every breath. With trembling hands, she wiped at the cold sweat that had gathered on her clammy brow, the sudden surge of adrenaline sending shivers down her spine.

The news report still echoed in her mind, haunting her like a malevolent specter. The John Doe burn victim, the enigma that had tormented her dreams, had awoken from his comatose state. And even more chilling was the revelation that this sinister figure, cloaked in mystery and darkness, had been identified as the infamous Boogeyman of Thornfield.

Amelia's fragile grip on reality faltered, threatening to slip away into the shadows. The medication, her only anchor in an unruly sea of delusions, seemed to have failed her on this fateful Christmas day. Panic surged within her, a tidal wave of terror threatening to consume her sanity whole.

She stumbled towards the bathroom, her legs weak and unreliable, as if the ground beneath her shifted and swayed like an unhinged funhouse floor. The memories of her own personal hell invaded her thoughts, clawing their way to the forefront of her tortured mind. The Boogeyman, a specter that had haunted her for years, lurking in the corners of her psyche, was now a tangible threat.

Amelia fell to her knees, retching violently into the porcelain toilet bowl. The sound of her own heaving filled the air, mingling with her anguished sobs. She could feel the darkness closing in, suffocating her senses, as if the Boogeyman had already laid claim to her fragile existence. The bathroom's harsh fluorescent light cast stark shadows on the walls, transforming the small space into a claustrophobic chamber of horrors.

As the acrid taste of vomit lingered in her mouth, her vision blurred and the world around her dimmed. Darkness engulfed her, the thick shroud of unconsciousness beckoning her deeper into its seductive embrace. In the vast expanse of the unconscious, Amelia's nightmares danced like demonic marionettes. She could hear the whispers, the sinister lullaby of her tormented mind. Images of a scarred face, seared flesh twisted into a mocking smile, invaded her dreamscape, suffusing it with terror.

And then, as if a switch had been flipped, Amelia's eyes fluttered open. The suffocating embrace of darkness was replaced by the harsh glare of reality. She blinked, her gaze slowly adjusting to the mundane familiarity of her surroundings. She found herself lying face down in her own vomit, the stench of her distress permeating the air. The nausea swelled within her, threatening to reclaim her weakened body. But as she struggled to push herself upright, a newfound resolve surged within her, an unwavering determination to confront the darkness that plagued her.

Amelia knew that if the Boogeyman had been released into the world, if he had stepped beyond the boundaries of her troubled mind, then she had no choice but to face him head-on. Armed with her medication and the flicker of hope that lingered within her shattered soul, she would battle the demons that sought to claim her.

For Amelia understood, with a clarity born from the depths of her own personal nightmare, that sometimes the monsters we fear most are the ones that reside within ourselves. And it was time to vanquish them, once and for all.

In the dimly lit living room of her parents' house, her mother and father sat quietly, their faces etched with concern. The news of the Boogeyman's awakening had spread like wildfire among their close-knit community, inflaming both fear and speculation. The usually festive ambiance of Christmas was replaced by an oppressive tension, hanging thick in the air like a storm cloud about to burst.

The phone rang incessantly, its shrill sound punctuating the silence with an almost menacing regularity. Each ring seemed to vibrate with the collective anxiety of those who knew Amelia's story, their voices tinged with worry and an unspoken question: What will happen next? Amelia's parents exchanged weary glances, their hearts heavy with the weight of their daughter's suffering.

Outside, snowflakes drifted down in a gentle cascade, blanketing the world in a deceptive calm. The holiday decorations that adorned their home seemed almost mocking in their cheerfulness, a stark contrast to the turmoil within. The twinkling lights and garlands, symbols of joy and celebration, did little to alleviate the dread that had settled over them.

Amelia's mother picked up the receiver, her hand trembling slightly as she answered yet another call from a concerned neighbor. The words exchanged were hollow, mere formalities masking the true depth of their collective fear. She assured them that Amelia was safe, though in her heart she knew that safety was a fleeting concept, easily shattered by the reappearance of the Boogeyman.

Meanwhile, Amelia stood in front of the bathroom mirror, her reflection a ghostly apparition. Her eyes, once vibrant and full of life, now held a haunted look, shadows of the nightmares that tormented her. She reached for the sink, turning on the cold water and splashing it onto her face, hoping to wash away the remnants of her terror. The water droplets clung to her skin like tears, each one a testament to her inner struggle.

As she gazed into the mirror, Amelia saw not just her reflection but the fractured pieces of her past. Each shard told a story of pain and resilience, of moments where she had fought against the darkness that threatened to consume her. She could see the scars, both visible and invisible, etched into her being by the relentless cruelty of the Boogeyman. But she also saw the flicker of defiance, a spark that had refused to be extinguished.

Amelia's resolve solidified, like steel tempered in the fires of her own anguish. She knew that she could not afford to falter, that she had to confront the Boogeyman not just for herself but for all those who had been affected by his malevolence. Her hands steadied, the trembling subsiding as determination took its place.

She reached for her medication, the pills a lifeline that helped anchor her in reality. As she swallowed them, she felt a semblance of control returning, a faint glimmer of hope piercing through the darkness. Amelia knew that this battle was far from over, but she was prepared to fight with every ounce of strength she possessed.

The living room remained cloaked in an uneasy silence, broken only by the occasional ring of the phone. Her parents' conversations continued, each call a reminder of the fragile hope that bound their community together. Despite their fear, they drew strength from each other, a silent vow to stand by Amelia's side no matter what lay ahead.

In the quiet aftermath of the calls, Amelia's parents sat together, their hands intertwined in a gesture of solidarity. They reflected on the journey that had brought them to this moment, the trials they had faced, and the resilience that had seen them through. Their love for Amelia was a beacon, guiding them through the darkest of times.

As the evening wore on, a sense of calm began to settle over the household. The oppressive tension that had gripped them slowly gave way to a tentative peace. The snow continued to fall outside, each flake a symbol of purity and renewal. Inside, the warmth of their love and support provided a sanctuary for Amelia, a place where she could find the strength to heal.

Amelia emerged from the bathroom, her steps more assured, her spirit fortified by the resolve she had found within herself. She joined her parents in the living room, their presence a balm to her wounded soul. Together, they faced the uncertainty of the future, united in their determination to overcome the shadows that had haunted them for so long.

In that quiet moment, surrounded by the love and support of her family, Amelia realized that she was not alone in her battle. The Boogeyman may have returned, but so had her strength and her will to fight. With her family by her side and the flicker of hope burning bright within her, she knew that she could face whatever came next.

The night stretched on, the promise of a new day lingering on the horizon. As Amelia looked out at the falling snow, she felt a sense of renewal, a belief that she could reclaim her life from the clutches of fear. The Boogeyman was a formidable foe, but Amelia was ready to confront him, to vanquish the darkness and find her way back to the light.

And so, in the dim light of that Christmas night, surrounded by the symbols of hope and renewal, Amelia took the first steps on her journey towards healing. The path ahead was fraught with challenges, but with the love of her family and the strength she had discovered within herself, she knew that she could overcome them. The Boogeyman's shadow would no longer dictate her fate, for Amelia had found the courage to face her fears and reclaim her life.

As the clock ticked towards midnight, the oppressive silence was shattered by the sharp, jarring ring of the phone. It pierced through the fragile calm like a siren, its insistent cry a reminder of the unresolved tension that still hung over them. Amelia's heart skipped a beat, her newfound resolve tested by this unexpected intrusion. Her parents exchanged anxious glances, the air thick with unspoken dread. The phone rang again, a relentless harbinger of the unknown, casting a long shadow over the fragile peace they had just begun to reclaim.

Chapter Twenty-Four

THE COLD, SHARP RING of the telephone shattered the uneasy silence, echoing through the dim-lit living room like the harbinger of an impending storm. Amelia's parents sat frozen, their eyes wide with a mixture of dread and disbelief, the room thick with an oppressive silence that seemed to scream with unspoken fears. The stark contrast between the peaceful white snow outside and the turmoil within their home created an unsettling paradox, as if the world beyond their windows was a tranquil facade masking the chaos within.

Her father couldn't help but tremble as he reached for the receiver, his fingers slipping slightly from the cold sweat that had gathered on his palms. The voices on the other end whispered with a mix of urgency and paranoia, each of them bearing the weight of an unspoken question: Would he seek revenge? Did he know about their involvement all those months ago?

Glancing at his wife, who wore a stoic expression fueled by fear, he fought to steady his trembling voice as he listened to the frantic whispers on the other end. The voices belonged to their co-conspirators, loyal allies in their attempt to protect their children from the darkness that had once consumed their lives.

His grip tightened on the armrest, his mind racing with countless unanswered questions. How had the Boogeyman survived that fateful night? The night they had collectively believed they had defeated him, banishing him to the depths of a coma-induced slumber. And now, as if mocking their feeble attempts to move on, he had emerged, hungry for vengeance.

Frustration mingled with his fear, a volatile cocktail of emotions threatening to consume him whole. But then he remembered their unanimous decision—the pact they had made in the face of this darkness. To play dumb and maintain silence, as painful and suffocating as it might be. They had to protect their loved ones, to shield them from the encroaching horrors that had been unleashed.

He replaced the receiver, the ringing now silent, a sense of grim determination filling the space between them. They would not succumb to panic, nor let the gnawing fear devour their sanity. They were survivors, no longer mere players in this wicked game. They may not have the answers, but they had each other.

As he sat back, the shadows in the room seemed to stretch and twist, morphing into the forms of old memories and half-forgotten fears. The Boogeyman's presence loomed over them, a dark cloud that refused to dissipate. But within that darkness, a flicker of defiance burned bright. They had faced him before and had emerged, if not victorious, then at least intact. They could do it again.

His wife moved closer, her hand finding his, the warmth of her touch grounding him amidst the swirling chaos of his thoughts. Together, they were stronger, their bond forged in the fires of past trials and tribulations. The Boogeyman might have returned, but so had their resolve to protect their family at all costs.

In that moment, a quiet understanding settled over them. They would face the Boogeyman, armed with the knowledge that they were not alone. The darkness may have awakened, but so had their determination. And as the clock ticked closer to midnight, they braced themselves for the storm that lay ahead, ready to face the Boogeyman and whatever twisted secrets he held within.

The phone sat silently on the table, a harbinger of the unknown. Each tick of the clock echoed through the room, a countdown to an uncertain future. The wind howled outside, rattling the windows and adding to the eerie atmosphere that seemed to envelop the house.

Amelia's parents sat in a silence heavy with anticipation, their minds whirling with the implications of that phone call.

They knew the Boogeyman was out there, somewhere, plotting his next move. The thought of him lurking in the shadows, waiting to strike, sent chills down their spines. But they refused to be paralyzed by fear. They had faced the darkness before, and they would do it again, no matter the cost.

The night stretched on, each minute feeling like an eternity. The oppressive tension in the room was almost palpable, a heavy weight pressing down on them. Yet, amid the fear and uncertainty, there was also a steely determination. They would not let the Boogeyman destroy their family. They would fight, tooth and nail, to protect what they held dear.

The phone rang again, its shrill tone piercing the silence. Amelia's father hesitated for a moment, his hand hovering over the receiver. He took a deep breath, steeling himself for whatever news lay on the other end of the line. With a resolute expression, he picked up the phone, ready to face whatever came next.

As he listened to the voice on the other end, his expression shifted from fear to resolve. The call was from another of their old allies, a reminder that they were not alone in this battle. They had support, a network of people who shared their fear and their determination. Together, they would stand against the Boogeyman, no matter what it took.

He hung up the phone, turning to his wife with a determined look in his eyes. He knew they were not alone in this. He made a mistake once, and now he would never let a thread of disgust cross the boundary of his home.

His wife nodded, her eyes filled with a mixture of fear and resolve. They had faced the Boogeyman before and had come out stronger. They could do it again. The phone's ring was not just a call to action but a reminder of their strength and unity. They would face the darkness together, armed with the knowledge that they were not alone.

In the stillness of the night, with the wind howling outside and the shadows closing in, they found solace in each other. The Boogeyman might be out there, but so was their resolve, burning bright against the encroaching darkness. They were ready for whatever came next, prepared to face their greatest fears with unwavering determination.

As the clock ticked towards midnight, the phone's silence echoed with the promise of impending challenges. But Amelia's parents sat together, hands intertwined, ready to confront the Boogeyman and whatever twisted secrets he held. The darkness had awakened, but so had their strength. They would face the storm head-on, united in their resolve to protect their family and overcome the shadows that threatened to consume them.

Chapter Twenty-Five

THE INCIDENT, AS THEY referred to it, had left them all trembling in its wake. They waited, day after agonizing day, for the Sheriff's cruiser to roll into town with the blaze of red and blue lights cutting through the night. The anticipation was a heavy cloud hanging over their lives, each moment stretching into an eternity as they envisioned the inevitable. They anticipated the handcuffs, the cold metal biting into their skin, ensuring they faced the twisted consequences of that night.

But it never came.

Days turned into weeks, weeks turned into months, and months turned into a year. The absence of justice was a devil's mockery, teasing them with false hope. The relief washed over them like a fever breaking, their collective sighs almost audible in the autumn air. They couldn't believe their luck, this miraculous escape from the clutches of fate.

The passing of time dulled the sharp edges of their fear, but a lingering sense of unease remained, like a persistent itch that couldn't be scratched. The town moved forward, its rhythm resuming with a hesitant normalcy. But fate, oh how she holds her cards close to her chest, waiting for the perfect moment to unleash her wicked hand. Life drifted on like a sluggish river, each resident desperately trying to paddle against the current, pretending that nothing had ever happened. They spoke of it in hushed whispers, wary of ears that might betray them. Surely, one of them had slipped up, left a breadcrumb they could follow, dragging them back to the scene of the crime.

Yet, the evidence remained hidden, buried deep within their secrets, taunting them for their transgression. The walls of Hawkins

Hollow seemed to hold the weight of their misdeeds, their very foundation shuddering under the burden of their deceit. Every brick and beam seemed to echo with the silent screams of their guilt, a chorus of whispers that only they could hear.

As the seasons passed, they grew bolder, emboldened by the clock's refusal to tick their demise. Their laughter echoed through the town square, their eyes gleaming with rejuvenated hope. The incident became nothing but a faint whisper in their minds, a phantom that had come and gone, its purpose served. The autumn leaves fell and were replaced by the blooms of spring, each cycle of nature a testament to their perceived reprieve.

But deep within, an unease gnawed at their souls, a slithering doubt that refused to be silenced. The shadows grew longer, darker, casting a foreboding presence upon the townsfolk. They exchanged knowing glances, recognizing the shared secret that bound them together in this twisted dance with destiny. Their conversations took on an edge, every word weighed with the potential to unravel their delicate facade.

For they knew, as surely as the moon waxes and wanes, that in the depths of the night, when the world is lost within its own nightmares, justice waits patiently. The Sheriff's cruiser might never roll into town, but the reckoning would come, delivered by the very hands of fate they had dared to defy. The wind whispered through the trees, a reminder of the promises that remained unfulfilled, the debts that had yet to be paid.

Their dreams were haunted by the specter of that night, the memories of their actions replaying with cruel clarity. The town's façade of peace and tranquility was a fragile shell, ready to crack under the weight of their collective guilt. The Boogeyman, a symbol of their darkest fears, lurked in the periphery of their vision, a constant reminder of the price of their silence.

As winter's chill gave way to spring's thaw, the town of Hawkins Hollow seemed to hold its breath. The air was thick with unspoken tension, the anticipation of an unseen storm. The residents moved through their days with a sense of foreboding, their laughter strained, their smiles brittle. They lived in the shadow of their past, each moment a reminder of the fragile balance they maintained.

The clock continued its relentless march, each tick a countdown to the inevitable. The Sheriff's absence was a cruel joke, the justice they feared a phantom that haunted their every waking moment. The nights were the worst, the darkness pressing in around them, amplifying their fears. The moonlight cast long shadows, transforming familiar shapes into menacing figures.

In the deepest part of the night, when sleep was elusive, they could almost hear the whispers of fate, promising that the reckoning was near. The quiet of their homes was filled with the echoes of their guilt, the creak of the floorboards a testament to the weight of their secrets. They knew they could not escape forever, that one day, the past would demand its due.

They waited, hearts pounding in the silence, for the day when their fragile peace would shatter. The tension was a living thing, a beast that prowled the edges of their consciousness, ready to pounce. They had bought themselves time, but at what cost? The price of their freedom was the constant gnawing of their souls, the knowledge that their actions had not gone unnoticed by the universe.

As the days turned into years, they clung to the hope that they could outlast the darkness, that their secrets would remain buried. But deep down, they knew the truth. Justice may be slow, but it is inexorable. The Boogeyman was out there, a silent judge waiting to pass sentence. And in the quiet moments, when they were alone with their thoughts, they could feel the weight of his gaze, a reminder that the past cannot be escaped, only confronted.

The residents of Thornfield lay in the grip of their fear, each day a delicate dance with fate. They had survived the initial storm, but the threat of the Boogeyman lingered, a shadow that could not be banished. They had no choice but to continue forward, one day at a time, hoping that when the reckoning came, they would have the strength to face it.

Chapter Twenty-Six

THE TOWN WHISPERED of a man who once lurked in the shadows, his malevolent deeds leaving scars deeper than flesh. He was a predator, preying on the innocence of children, a true embodiment of evil. But even the wicked must face the consequences of their actions. Fate dealt him a cruel hand, as he was caught in the fiery grasp of retribution. Yet, the question lingered: could the atrocities committed against him ever truly balance the scales of justice? Could the torment he endured serve as a fitting retribution for the lives he shattered? As the flames consumed him, leaving behind a shell of his former self, the town was left to ponder if justice had been served, or if the cycle of violence had merely continued.

In the back of his mind, he thought he would get away with his wrongdoings. As he stared at his reflection in the mirror, the scars that once marred his face and body were now merely reminders of the dark forces that had consumed his existence. The fire had taken so much from him, and he had paid the price in pain and suffering. The memories of his heinous acts, those unspeakable crimes against innocence, were etched in his soul, branding him as the Boogeyman who once prowled the shadows, preying on the vulnerable.

The doctors had worked tirelessly to restore some semblance of humanity to his disfigured form. Countless skin grafts and surgeries had pieced him back together, each painful stitch a reminder of the torment he had endured. But though his physical wounds had healed, the scars ran deeper, etched into the very fabric of his being. He was a patchwork of flesh and nightmares, a grotesque reminder of the darkness he had inflicted upon others.

There were two years spent in the confines of a sterile hospital, undergoing procedure after procedure to salvage what was left of his appearance. And then there were the grueling years of rehabilitation, each step an agonizing reminder of the agony he had been through. He had learned to walk again, albeit with the aid of a crutch, but he knew he would never truly be whole. Each day was a battle, his body a battleground of pain and resilience, his mind a labyrinth of guilt and terror.

The fire had robbed him of his physical strength, leaving him dependent on the support of a cold, inanimate object. But it had taken more than just his physical prowess; it had preyed on his sanity, leaving him forever changed. Nightmares haunted his every moment, as though the flames had consumed not just his flesh, but his mind as well. The faces of his victims, those innocent souls, haunted his dreams, their eyes accusing, their voices a relentless chorus of torment.

Now, as he stood on the threshold between a past stained with darkness and an uncertain future, he yearned for one thing above all else – anonymity. The former monster that had once prowled the shadows, inflicting terror upon innocent souls, was now a scarred figure attempting to blend into the backdrop of society. He longed to disappear, to become a mere shadow in the crowd, unnoticed and unremarkable.

He took solace in the fact that the surgeries and grafts had distorted his appearance enough that he could pass, perhaps, as just another survivor of life's cruel trials. In a world where appearances were often deceptive, he hoped no one would recognize the twisted creature that lay beneath the surface. He wore his disfigurement like a mask, a shield against the probing eyes of those who might see the darkness that still lurked within him.

It was a constant battle, to hold on to the shreds of his sanity, to overcome the anguish that threatened to consume him. Each day, he ventured out into the world once more, relying on his ever-present companion, the crutch. Yet, the shadows that clung to his soul would forever remind him of his diabolical nature. The crutch was not just a physical support; it was a symbol of his brokenness, a reminder of the sins that had crippled his spirit.

As he navigated the crowded streets, the whispers of the past followed him, a ghostly chorus that he could not escape. He saw the world through a veil of regret, each face a mirror reflecting his guilt. The innocent laughter of children was a knife to his heart, a painful reminder of the lives he had shattered. He kept his head down, avoiding eye contact, fearing that someone might see through his disguise, might recognize the monster behind the mask.

In the dim light of his small apartment, he would sit for hours, lost in the labyrinth of his thoughts. The walls seemed to close in on him, the silence a suffocating blanket that smothered his screams. He was a prisoner of his own mind, shackled by the weight of his sins. The faces of his victims haunted him, their eyes pleading for justice, their voices a relentless echo of his guilt.

Every knock on the door, every unexpected sound, sent waves of panic through his body. He lived in constant fear of discovery, the dread that the world would one day remember the Boogeyman and drag him back into the abyss. The newspapers had long forgotten his crimes, but he knew that the memory of his deeds would never fade from his mind. He was a man marked by his past, his soul scarred by the evil he had unleashed.

In the darkest hours of the night, when sleep eluded him, he would stare into the mirror, confronting the monster he had become. The reflection was a stranger, a grotesque parody of the man he once was. The scars were a map of his sins, each line a testament to the pain he had inflicted. He would trace them with trembling fingers, feeling the ridges and valleys of his guilt.

He sought redemption in the small acts of kindness, trying to balance the scales of his soul. He would help the elderly cross the street, donate anonymously to charities, volunteer at shelters. But no matter how many good deeds he performed, the darkness within him could not be erased. It was a stain that would never wash away, a shadow that would always follow him.

The world around him continued to turn, indifferent to his internal struggle. People passed him by, oblivious to the storm raging within his heart. He envied their ignorance, their blissful unawareness of the horrors that walked among them. He longed to scream, to confess his sins, to beg for forgiveness. But he knew that his words would fall on deaf ears, that the world had no mercy for monsters like him.

As the years went by, the lines on his face deepened, the weight of his guilt growing heavier with each passing day. He moved through life like a ghost, invisible and forgotten. The Boogeyman was a specter of the past, a nightmare that had faded from memory. But for him, the horror was eternal, the flames of his sins burning bright in the depths of his soul.

He had always known that he would never live a normal life again. The scars were a reminder of the darkness that had consumed him, the fire a punishment for his sins. He was a man condemned to walk the earth, haunted by the ghosts of his past, forever seeking redemption in a world that had moved on. The Boogeyman might have disappeared from the headlines, but he would never escape the prison of his own making.

Chapter Twenty-Seven

AMELIA SLOWLY CLOSED her laptop, the weight of her achievement settling deep within her chest like a precious stone. Four years had unfolded in a whirlwind of relentless determination, nights spent poring over textbooks, and days punctuated by therapy sessions that were both her lifeline and her crucible. Graduating with a degree in psychology was not just an academic triumph; it was a testament to her resilience in the face of unspeakable horrors.

The trauma she had endured, the tendrils of nightmares that still occasionally wrapped themselves around her consciousness, had threatened to pull her under countless times. They whispered insidiously in her ear, weaving doubts and fear into the fabric of her being. Yet, Amelia refused to surrender to their haunting embrace. With every therapy session, with every pill swallowed to calm her racing thoughts, she ventured further away from the crumbling ruins of her past.

They called her brave, but Amelia knew the truth. Behind her composed exterior, stitched together by therapy and medication, fear still clawed at her heart like a relentless predator. The Boogeyman, the monstrous specter that had once consumed her entire existence, had been rendered a mere shadow of his former self in reality. Rumors whispered across town of his descent into helplessness, yet Amelia's mind still painted his face in the darkest corners, a constant reminder of what she had survived.

Forget it, she would tell herself bitterly. The memories, the scars still etched in her soul, could not be erased so easily. No matter how much time passed or how far she distanced herself from it all, the

Boogeyman's lingering presence refused to fade. Every darkened hallway, every unlit room became a battlefield of her own making, where shadows danced with memories and fear lurked in the unseen corners.

But Amelia was determined to reclaim her life, to forge a path towards normalcy that had once seemed an impossible dream. College had been her sanctuary, a realm where she could bury herself in the depths of knowledge and escape the suffocating grip of her past. Online classes had been a lifeline to the outside world when venturing beyond her safe haven seemed daunting and insurmountable. Slowly, she had gathered enough courage to step onto campus, to face the real-world interactions that had once triggered paralyzing anxiety.

Though trust still eluded her grasp like a slippery fish, Amelia had made undeniable progress. She had conquered the demons of her own mind, wrestled with the shadows that threatened to swallow her whole. She refused to let them define her or dictate her future. With each passing day, she grew stronger, more resilient in the face of her inner turmoil. And yet, the Boogeyman's face remained, an indelible mark etched into her psyche, a constant reminder of the battles she had fought and the war she had waged within herself.

There were moments, fleeting and unexpected, when she felt the tendrils of darkness threaten to overcome her once more. The memories would surface like specters from the depths, triggering panic and despair. But like a phoenix rising from the ashes of her past, Amelia refused to be engulfed by the monsters within. She had learned to navigate the labyrinth of her trauma with a fragile grace, acknowledging her scars as part of her story without allowing them to define her destiny.

In the quiet moments between classes, Amelia would find solace in the rhythm of her own heartbeat, a steady cadence that anchored her amidst the tumult of university life. She sought refuge in the campus library, where the scent of old books and the hushed whispers of knowledge seekers provided a sanctuary of peace. Here, she could lose herself in the labyrinthine stacks, burying her fears beneath layers of academic pursuit and intellectual curiosity.

Her professors had become unwitting mentors in her journey of healing, their words of encouragement and guidance a balm to her wounded spirit. They saw beyond the scars that marked her exterior, recognizing the resilience and determination that burned brightly within. In their lectures and discussions, Amelia found not just academic enlightenment but a sense of belonging that had eluded her for so long.

As graduation day approached, anticipation mingled with apprehension in Amelia's heart. The ceremony would mark the culmination of years of hard work and personal triumphs, a celebration of her journey from victim to survivor. Yet, beneath the veneer of achievement, uncertainty lingered. The Boogeyman's ghost still haunted her dreams, a reminder that healing was not a linear path but a series of peaks and valleys.

Amelia knew that the road ahead would be fraught with challenges that the scars of her past would continue to shape her present and future. But she had come too far to turn back now. With each step across the stage on graduation day, she would carry with her not just a diploma but a testament to her strength and resilience. The Boogeyman's legacy would forever be a part of her story, but it would not define the chapters yet to be written.

In the days leading up to graduation, Amelia found herself reflecting on the journey that had brought her to this pivotal moment. She revisited the memories she had once tried to bury deep within, facing them with a newfound clarity and determination. The therapy sessions, the sleepless nights, the moments of crippling fear—they had all been stepping stones on her path to reclaiming her life.

She thought back to the first time she had stepped foot on campus, her heart pounding with a mixture of excitement and dread. The halls had seemed vast and unfamiliar, echoing with the chatter of students who navigated their way with ease. For Amelia, each step had felt like crossing a treacherous bridge suspended over a chasm of uncertainty. But she had persisted, drawing strength from the support of her therapists, her professors, and the inner resilience that had carried her through the darkest of times.

The library had become her refuge, a sanctuary where she could immerse herself in the world of psychology, dissecting theories and exploring the complexities of the human mind. Among the towering shelves of books, she had found solace in knowledge, a tangible anchor amidst the intangible fears that still haunted her. The musty scent of old pages had mingled with the aroma of determination, fueling her quest for understanding and healing.

In her final year, as she delved deeper into her studies, Amelia had encountered moments of doubt and self-doubt. The Boogeyman's face would surface unexpectedly, a chilling reminder of the trauma that had once threatened to consume her. But with each passing day, she had grown more adept at confronting her fears, recognizing them as echoes of a past she was determined to transcend.

The support of her professors had been instrumental in her journey. They had seen beyond the scars that marked her skin, recognizing the resilience and courage that defined her character. Their words of encouragement had bolstered her confidence, reminding her that she was more than the sum of her traumas.

As graduation day dawned, Amelia found herself standing on the threshold of a new chapter, poised to embrace the future with renewed hope and determination. The ceremony was a celebration of not just academic achievement but of personal triumph over adversity. As she walked across the stage to receive her diploma, applause echoing around her, she felt a surge of pride and gratitude.

The trauma she endured would forever be a part of her story, a testament to the resilience and strength that had carried her through the darkest of times. But as she looked to the future, Amelia knew that she was more than a survivor—she was a thriver, ready to carve out a life filled with purpose and possibility.

Chapter Twenty-Eight

AMELIA HAD ALWAYS CRAVED freedom, an elusive beacon beckoning her to spread her wings and escape the suffocating weight of her past in Thornfield. When the opportunity finally presented itself in the form of a charming duplex nestled in the quaint town of Hawkins Hollow, she seized it without hesitation. Living under the watchful eyes of the Boogeyman had felt like being a caged bird yearning for the open sky, and this move promised a fresh start, a chance to reclaim her autonomy.

The duplex, with its weathered wood and faded paint, exuded a quaint charm that drew Amelia in from the moment she first laid eyes on it. Yet, beneath its seemingly innocuous exterior, there lingered an unsettling aura—an unspoken history that whispered tales of tragedy and despair to anyone who dared to listen. Amelia, however, blinded by the allure of newfound freedom, remained blissfully unaware of the shadows that lurked within the very walls she now called home.

As she settled into her new abode, the walls seemed to murmur secrets carried on the soft breeze that swept through the town. The ancient timbers groaned with stories untold, their echoes reverberating through the rooms like ghostly whispers. But Amelia, enraptured by the taste of liberation, brushed aside the subtle warnings that danced on the edges of her consciousness.

Night after night, as she drifted into slumber nestled in the comforting embrace of her new sanctuary, her dreams took on a vivid and disconcerting hue. Scenes unfolded like sinister vignettes, woven with threads of unease that left her waking in a cold sweat, heart racing against the silence of the night. The line between dreams and reality began to blur, until the veil separating the two realms grew thin and fragile.

The nightmares that once haunted only her sleep began to encroach upon her waking hours. Shadows, once benign, now took on a sinister life of their own, flickering at the periphery of her vision like will-o'-the-wisp. They tugged at her sanity with invisible tendrils, casting doubt on what was real and what was imagined. Amelia found herself caught in a relentless dance with her own fears, each step leading her deeper into a labyrinth of uncertainty.

Her newfound freedom, initially a beacon of hope, had metamorphosed into a gilded cage. The duplex, once a symbol of liberation and independence, now stood as a stark reminder of the darkness that lurked within her own mind. The very walls seemed to close in around her, their presence oppressive and suffocating.

Amelia's yearning for freedom had evolved, twisted by the realities she had not anticipated. Now, she longed not just for escape from the confines of Thornfield and the specter of the Boogeyman but for a return to the safety and familiarity of her parents' protective embrace. The life she had once scorned now beckoned to her like a distant beacon in the storm, offering solace and security amidst the unknown terrors of Hawkins Hollow.

In the daylight hours, as she navigated the quaint streets of her new town, Amelia tried to find solace in the small comforts that surrounded her. The local café, with its steaming cups of coffee and friendly chatter, provided a brief respite from the shadows that plagued her thoughts. She sought refuge in the pages of books borrowed from the town library, losing herself in stories that offered fleeting escape from the gnawing unease that had taken root within her.

But the nights remained her greatest adversary, when the darkness descended like a heavy shroud and the whispers of the duplex's walls grew louder and more insistent. Sleep became a fleeting luxury, each night fraught with the anticipation of haunting dreams that would wrench her from slumber in a clamor of fear and confusion.

Amelia knew, deep down, that the battle she faced was not just against the external forces that surrounded her but against the inner demons that threatened to consume her. The trauma of her past had left scars that ran deeper than any physical wound, scars that pulsed with a rawness that refused to be ignored. She had hoped that Hawkins Hollow would offer sanctuary, a haven where she could rebuild her shattered life. Instead, it had become a battleground where her courage and resilience were tested with each passing day.

As the weeks turned into months, Amelia found herself grappling with questions that had no easy answers. Was the darkness she sensed within the duplex a manifestation of her own fears, or did it hold secrets that defied rational explanation? Could she ever truly find peace in a place haunted by shadows, or was she destined to forever be ensnared in a web of terror and uncertainty?

The townspeople, with their polite smiles and guarded gazes, offered no solace. They seemed to carry secrets of their own, their whispers and sidelong glances adding to the atmosphere of unease that permeated Hawkins Hollow. Amelia sensed that she was an outsider here, a newcomer whose presence stirred dormant echoes and threatened to disturb the delicate balance of the town's quiet façade.

Yet, amid the uncertainty and fear, Amelia found moments of unexpected clarity. She discovered strength in the vulnerability she had once feared, courage in the face of the unknown. Each day brought new challenges, new opportunities to confront the shadows that threatened to overwhelm her. And though the road ahead remained fraught with obstacles, Amelia vowed to navigate it with a steadfast resolve born of survival and resilience.

The duplex, with its weathered façade and whispered secrets, stood as a symbol of her journey—a testament to the courage it took to confront the darkness within and the determination to forge a path toward light. As she stood on the threshold of uncertainty, Amelia knew that the battles she faced were not just hers alone. They were battles fought by countless others who had dared to confront their own demons, who had refused to surrender to the darkness that sought to engulf them.

In the depths of night, when the world lay cloaked in darkness and silence, Amelia wrestled with her fears. She traced the patterns of moonlight that filtered through the curtains, casting ethereal shadows across the room. And in those solitary moments, she found a glimmer of hope—a flicker of resilience that burned brightly amidst the encroaching darkness.

The journey ahead would be arduous, filled with moments of doubt and despair. But Amelia had tasted freedom, however fleeting, and she was determined to hold onto it with every ounce of strength she possessed. The duplex, with its faded paint and weathered wood, had become her battleground—a place where she would confront her deepest fears and reclaim the sense of peace that had eluded her for so long.

As dawn broke over Hawkins Hollow, casting its gentle light upon the sleepy town, Amelia stood at her window and watched the world awaken. The shadows retreated, if only temporarily, giving way to the promise of a new day. And as she breathed in the crisp morning air, she felt a sense of quiet resolve settle within her—a reminder that, despite the darkness that surrounded her, she possessed the strength to face whatever lay ahead.

For Amelia had always yearned for freedom, and now, in the heart of Hawkins Hollow, she would discover that true liberation lay not in escaping the shadows but in confronting them head-on.

Chapter Twenty-Nine

AMELIA HAD BELIEVED, with a fervent hope born of resilience, that she had outgrown the terror that once gripped her childhood. The nightmares, once vivid and consuming, had become faded echoes buried deep within the recesses of her mind. Moving into the duplex in Hawkins Hollow had seemed like the perfect escape, a sanctuary where the haunting specters of her past could finally be exorcised.

Yet, any semblance of peace and tranquility swiftly proved to be nothing more than a mirage—a cruel illusion that lulled Amelia into a false sense of security. As days stretched into weeks, an insidious unease coiled around her like tendrils of smoke, tightening its grip on her fragile sanity. Like a relentless predator, the Boogeyman had returned, his presence looming larger with each passing night, ready to unleash his torment upon her once more.

It began subtly, with faint whispers that crept into the stillness of the night like ghostly murmurs. Shadows danced on the walls of her bedroom, their undulating movements akin to an eerie tango, mocking Amelia's attempts at normalcy. She shivered involuntarily, unable to shake off the persistent feeling that she was not alone—that some malevolent force lurked just beyond her field of vision, poised to engulf her in darkness once again.

Her once-cozy bedroom, now transformed into a claustrophobic chamber of dread, seemed to conspire against her. The closet door creaked open with agonizing slowness, as though taunting her with its ominous sounds, releasing a palpable aura of menace. From its depths, a sinister presence emerged—the Boogeyman himself, his lurid eyes dripping with malice, leering at Amelia from within the confines of her own home.

Each night became a battleground for her sanity, fraught with hideous visions that tormented her with images too ghastly to describe. In the depths of darkness, she would awaken drenched in sweat, her heart pounding against her ribcage as if desperate to escape its fleshy prison. It was a war for her very soul, a harrowing struggle against the demons that had taken root within the walls of her duplex.

Desperation clawed at her, urging her to confront the ancient terror that had haunted her since childhood. Memories long suppressed surged back with devastating force, flooding her senses with a crippling wave of fear that threatened to engulf her once more. The Boogeyman, it seemed, defied the boundaries of time and space, his malevolent presence permeating every corner of her existence, even when she believed she had escaped his clutches.

In the heart-stopping climax that would test her resolve, Amelia would confront the Boogeyman in a battle for her very survival. Amidst the chilling tableau of their unsettling dance, she would come to a profound realization—that the true horror lay not solely in the monster itself, but in the depths of her own psyche. The Boogeyman existed as a manifestation of her deepest fears, a grotesque reflection of her insecurities and vulnerabilities.

For in Hawkins Hollow, darkness was not merely a backdrop but a living, breathing entity—an entity that taunted, tormented, and tested the limits of human resilience. The echoes of its haunting presence lingered in the minds of its inhabitants, whispering tales of the Boogeyman that lurked within the darkest recesses of their own closets.

As the days wore on, Amelia wrestled with existential questions that defied easy answers. Was the terror she faced a tangible force or a projection of her own fractured psyche? Could she ever truly escape the clutches of her past, or was she destined to be forever ensnared in a cycle of fear and uncertainty?

The townspeople, with their guarded gazes and masked whispers, offered little solace. They seemed to carry secrets of their own, their faces betraying glimpses of fear and suspicion that mirrored Amelia's own turmoil. In their eyes, she saw reflections of her own struggle—a silent acknowledgment of the darkness that lurked beneath the surface of Hawkins Hollow.

Yet, amidst the prevailing sense of dread, Amelia discovered unexpected reservoirs of strength. She unearthed courage in the face of overwhelming adversity, resilience in the shadow of despair. Each day became a testament to her unwavering determination to confront the demons that threatened to consume her—to reclaim her sense of peace and autonomy in a town where shadows danced at the edges of reality.

The duplex, once a symbol of escape and new beginnings, now stood as a crucible where Amelia would confront her deepest fears. Its weathered façade and whispered secrets bore witness to her journey—a journey fraught with peril and uncertainty, yet illuminated by moments of profound self-discovery.

In the darkness of night, when the world lay cloaked in silence, Amelia grappled with her fears. She traced the patterns of moonlight that filtered through her window, casting ethereal shadows across the room. And in those solitary moments, she found a glimmer of hope—a flicker of resilience that burned brightly amidst the encroaching darkness.

The road ahead remained fraught with challenges and obstacles, yet Amelia refused to succumb to despair. She had tasted freedom, however fleeting, and she was determined to hold onto it with every fiber of her being. The duplex, with its faded paint and haunted corridors, had become her battleground—a place where she would confront the Boogeyman and, in doing so, confront the darkest corners of her own soul.

As dawn broke over Hawkins Hollow, bathing the town in the gentle embrace of morning light, Amelia stood at her window and watched the world awaken. The shadows receded, if only temporarily, yielding to the promise of a new day. And as she breathed in the crisp morning air, she felt a sense of quiet resolve settle within her—a reminder that, despite the darkness that surrounded her, she possessed the strength to face whatever lay ahead.

For Amelia had thought she had outgrown the terror that once consumed her. Yet, in the heart of Hawkins Hollow, she would come to realize that true liberation lay not in fleeing from fear but in confronting it head-on—in embracing the shadows that threatened to engulf her and emerging stronger on the other side.

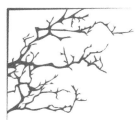

Chapter Thirty

AMELIA'S NIGHTS HAD devolved into a treacherous maze, a labyrinthine nightmare where the Boogeyman prowled with malicious intent, waiting to ensnare her sanity. It began subtly, with flickering shadows that danced upon her bedroom walls like ghostly apparitions, their movements weaving a chilling symphony from the darkest corners of the universe.

In the fragile hours before dawn, she would awaken drenched in sweat, her heart racing as if trying to flee the relentless pursuit of fear. Clutching her chest, Amelia struggled to contain the rampant palpitations that threatened to overwhelm her fragile composure. It was the Boogeyman, she knew, his presence palpable yet intangible, lurking ever closer, relishing the terror he had instilled within her.

Haunted by the monstrous specter that had taken residence within her mind, Amelia reluctantly sought solace in the sterile confines of her doctor's office. The clinical environment, though ostensibly calm, seemed to pulse with an undercurrent of unease. The pale yellow walls, bathed in the sterile glow of fluorescent lights, whispered secrets that echoed ominously in her ears.

Her doctor listened attentively, his expression a mask of professional concern as Amelia poured forth her shattered emotions onto the worn leather couch. Behind him, a stack of medical journals stood sentinel, their spines rigid as if poised to expose her vulnerabilities to the lurking shadows of her past.

Relief washed over her in a fleeting wave, a temporary respite from the relentless torment that plagued her nights. Her doctor swiftly prescribed a regimen of medication, urging her to adhere to it religiously. He promised that the pills would quell the feeling of impending doom that haunted her mind—erasing the whispers and nightmares that threatened to consume her existence.

Days blurred into nights, the pale glow of the moon casting an ethereal pallor upon Amelia's bedroom. She swallowed the prescribed medication dutifully, clinging to the hope that it would silence the relentless whispers and banish the specter of the Boogeyman that haunted her every thought. Yet, with each passing night, the grip of fear tightened around her like a suffocating veil, its claws sinking deeper into her fragile psyche.

Desperation enveloped her like an icy shroud, driving her once again to the threshold of her doctor's office. This time, his analytical gaze bore a hint of frustration—a crack in his professional façade that hinted at his own vulnerability in the face of the all-encompassing darkness that gripped Amelia's mind.

Her heart pounded in her chest, torn between hope and despair. Was the answer truly to be found in medication alone, or was there a deeper truth she had yet to confront? Was the Boogeyman merely a manifestation of the shadows she had long refused to acknowledge—the embodiment of fears buried deep within her subconscious?

The doctor's voice, measured and calm, resonated in the sterile silence of the room as he adjusted his glasses and met her gaze. Her doctor would tell her that sometimes the path to healing lies not in masking our fears, but in confronting them head-on. Medication can provide temporary relief, but true healing requires us to delve into the depths of our own psyche.

His words echoed in her mind as she left the office, a seed of doubt planted amidst the turmoil of her thoughts. Could she find the courage to confront the Boogeyman—to unravel the tangled web of fears that bound her to the shadows? Or would she remain trapped in a cycle of medication and fleeting relief, forever haunted by the specter of her own insecurities?

That night, as darkness descended upon Hawkins Hollow, Amelia stood at her bedroom window and gazed out at the moonlit landscape. The shadows danced on the periphery of her vision, whispering secrets that she strained to comprehend. In the depths of her soul, a flicker of resolve ignited—a spark of determination to confront the Boogeyman and reclaim her peace of mind.

For in the heart of her own darkness, Amelia understood that true liberation awaited not in avoidance, but in the courageous act of facing her deepest fears. The journey ahead would be fraught with uncertainty and peril, yet she was determined to walk that path—to confront the Boogeyman and, in doing so, to discover the strength and resilience that lay dormant within her own heart.

Chapter Thirty-One

AMIDST THE FLICKERING shadows, shattered glass, and the cries of a family on the edge, Amelia's parents embarked on a harrowing quest to save their beloved girl. The duplex, once a sanctuary, now resembled a twisted maze of desperation and paranoia.

As they tore through the rooms, flipping furniture and ripping open drawers, they could almost taste the insidious presence lurking in the darkness. Every creak of a floorboard sent shivers down their spines, echoing the Boogeyman's wicked laughter. They were consumed by a fervor, an unyielding determination to root out the evil that held their daughter captive.

Amelia's father, a stern man with worry etched deep into his weathered face, tore through the attic in a frenzied frenzy. The dust particles danced in the pale moonlight that seeped through the cobweb-covered windows. He scanned the space with an intensity matched only by the Boogeyman himself, his heart pounding in his chest like the drums of doom.

Meanwhile, her mother, a woman of unwavering love and tenacity, traversed the basement. The cold, damp air clung to her skin, provoking goosebumps to rise like soldiers at attention. She moved among the shadows, her flashlight casting eerie shadows on the grimy walls. With each step, she prayed to any deity that might be listening, beseeching them to guide her to the key that would unlock her daughter's salvation.

The search seemed endless, the passage of time non-existent. In a fusion of fear and love, Amelia's parents clung to the hope that somewhere, within the vast expanse of the duplex, they would find the catalyst of their daughter's torment. With each failed attempt, their spirits wavered, like a flickering flame threatened by an unforgiving gust of wind.

Chapter Thirty-Two

THE AIR WAS THICK WITH the suffocating stench of fear, saturating every crevice of their beings. With hearts pounding in unison, Amelia's parents pressed on, their determination a beacon in the swirling darkness. Shadows seemed to leap and twist with a life of their own, playing tricks on their minds as they navigated the treacherous path ahead. Every creak of the floorboards echoed like a chilling warning, urging them to quicken their pace. Yet, in the face of uncertainty, they clung to hope like a lifeline, refusing to succumb to the encroaching terror. Each step forward was a defiance against the Boogeyman's eternal grasp, a testament to a parent's unyielding love.

With adrenaline coursing through their veins, a fiery blend of terror and resolve propelling them forward, they surged through the house like warriors charging into the heart of a tempest. Each room became a battleground, where every overturned chair and hastily opened drawer held the potential to unveil the secrets needed to free Amelia from her torment. The urgency of their mission turned every movement into a frantic dance, as if time itself were an enemy to be outwitted.

Every creak of the floorboards sent a chill down their spines, a haunting reminder of the Boogeyman's mocking presence lurking in the shadows. His laughter seemed to echo through the very structure of their home, a malevolent symphony that fueled their determination even as it filled them with dread. Theirs was a race against the clock, a struggle that tested their courage and resourcefulness with each passing moment.

Amelia's father, a stern man whose face bore the weight of worry etched deep into weathered lines, ascended into the attic with a fervor matched only by the mythical monster they sought. The attic, cloaked in shadows and cobwebs, greeted him with dust particles dancing in the pale moonlight that filtered through small, grimy windows. His breath came in ragged bursts, the air thick with anticipation and dread as he scanned the forgotten relics stored in the attic's depths. Each item held potential, each corner a potential hiding place for the lurking evil that threatened to consume their daughter's soul.

The attic's eerie silence was broken only by the rustling of old newspapers and the occasional scuttle of rodents in hiding. Boxes stacked haphazardly seemed to teeter on the brink of revealing their long-held secrets. Amelia's father meticulously searched through each crate, his hands trembling as he unearthed forgotten childhood toys, dusty books with faded covers, and a collection of old photographs that whispered stories of times long past. With each discovery, his heart sank deeper into despair, for none provided the elusive clue that could lead to Amelia's rescue.

Meanwhile, Amelia's mother, a woman of unwavering love and tenacity, descended into the basement—a cold, clammy abyss that clung to her like a suffocating embrace. The dim beam of her flashlight sliced through the darkness, casting long, distorted shadows that seemed to dance mockingly on the grimy walls. Her heart hammered in her chest, her footsteps echoing in the stillness as she navigated the labyrinthine passages of the basement. Each step forward felt like a leap of faith, as she pleaded silently to any deity who might be listening, beseeching them to guide her to the elusive key that would unlock her daughter's salvation.

The basement, with its low ceilings and musty scent, held secrets of its own—a jumble of forgotten belongings, discarded furniture, and cobwebs that draped like mournful curtains. Amelia's mother pushed through the chill that seeped into her bones, her mind racing with memories of Amelia's laughter echoing through these same walls. Her fingers brushed against dusty boxes and old tools, their presence a testament to the mundane yet unsettling silence that pervaded the basement's atmosphere.

Time blurred into an agonizing continuum as they searched, the seconds stretching into eternity with each failed attempt to uncover the source of Amelia's torment. The duplex, once a place of refuge, now seemed to conspire against them—a puzzle with pieces scattered beyond their reach. Yet, fueled by a love that transcended the barriers of fear and doubt, they persisted. Their spirits flickered like a fragile flame threatened by the gusts of uncertainty, yet they refused to yield.

In their valiant mission to save Amelia, they faced not only the palpable darkness cloaking their home but also the murky depths of their own psyches. Each step forward, each hidden corner explored, unraveled layers of their deepest fears and vulnerabilities, laying bare their inner struggles in the face of external terror. The Boogeyman, a sinister embodiment of childhood nightmares, now loomed as a manifestation of the collective dread threatening to engulf them all.

As they meticulously combed through the duplex, their resolve faltered, tested by the unyielding onslaught of doubt and weariness. In the heart of Hawkins Hollow, where darkness danced unchecked, the battle for Amelia's soul had only just ignited, casting their courage against the relentless shadows that sought to consume them.

Chapter Thirty-Three

AS THEY HUDDLED TOGETHER, the flickering images on the screen cast a chilling pall over the room, each frame unfolding like a macabre tale etched in shadows. The tape played before their eyes, revealing the unsettling choreography of Amelia's neighbor as he prowled through the labyrinthine attic of the duplex. His movements were stealthy, a predator navigating the darkness with eerie precision, his figure hauntingly silhouetted against the dim light filtering through cobwebbed windows.

Amelia's breath caught in her throat as the footage edged closer to her side of the duplex. The attic, once a forgotten space steeped in benign neglect, now loomed as a theater of dread. She watched with a growing sense of unease as the neighbor slipped through the narrow entrance leading into her closet—a violation of her sanctuary, where her most intimate belongings lay ensconced. What had compelled him to breach these sacred boundaries? What sinister purpose had driven him to invade the privacy of her personal space?

Fear coiled like a serpent in her stomach, tightening its grip with each passing second. The attic, once a realm of forgotten treasures and dust-covered relics, had become a stage for the neighbor's clandestine activities. His presence lingered like a stalking butler, casting a shadow that seemed to stretch across the room even after the tape had stopped playing.

Amelia's father wasted no time in alerting the authorities. The police arrived swiftly, their demeanor grim and purposeful as they took in the gravity of the situation. They gathered around the screen in solemn silence, their expressions a mirror of the horror and disbelief that washed over them with each revelation on the tape. What had been mere suspicion and unease now solidified into incontrovertible evidence of a nefarious scheme unfolding right under their noses.

The handcuffs clicked around the neighbor's wrists with a finality that echoed through the room. Immobilized and subdued, he stood as a chilling testament to the darkness that lurks within the hearts of men. Yet, for all the apprehension and closure this arrest brought, the true depths of the horrors were yet to be unearthed.

Armed with a warrant, the police descended upon the neighbor's house—a seemingly ordinary residence that now stood as a monument to the grotesque. The air inside hung heavy with a palpable sense of foreboding, as though the walls themselves harbored secrets too sinister to be contained. The officers moved with cautious determination, their flashlights cutting through the oppressive darkness that clung to the hallway like a shroud.

What awaited them inside was a tableau of madness—a grim tapestry woven with threads of depravity and malice. The walls, once adorned with the mundane trappings of suburban life, now bore witness to a grotesque gallery of photographs. Faces of unsuspecting residents stared back with eyes scratched out in a frenzy of deranged fury, a testament to the neighbor's twisted obsession.

The stench of decay mingled with the acrid air, assaulting their senses as they ventured deeper into the dreary corridors of the house. In a hidden chamber concealed behind a false wall, they made a chilling discovery—a collection of bones meticulously arranged like trophies upon a macabre altar. Each skeletal fragment whispered of lives snuffed out, of innocence violated and extinguished by the neighbor's insatiable appetite for darkness.

The officers stood transfixed, their minds struggling to reconcile the banality of suburban life with the horrors laid bare before them. The neighbor, now detained and shackled, offered no explanation for his grotesque tableau. His eyes, vacant and devoid of remorse, bore witness to a mind unhinged—a mind that had descended into the abyss of depravity, where morality and humanity had long since been eclipsed by the shadows.

Outside, the night pressed against the windows like a black hole, as if seeking entry into this house of horrors. The officers exchanged solemn glances, their hearts heavy with the weight of what they had witnessed. For in this quiet corner of the world, where neighbors exchanged pleasantries and children played in the streets, a darkness had taken root—a darkness that defied reason and gnawed at the edges of sanity.

As they secured the scene and prepared to remove the neighbor and his grisly trophies from the house, a chilling realization settled over them like a winter fog. The nightmares that would haunt them in the days and weeks to come were not condemned to the confines of this house alone. The true horror lay in the realization that such darkness could reside in the most unassuming of places, lurking behind closed doors and within the hearts of those who walk among us, concealed by masks of normalcy.

In the aftermath of that fateful night, as the town grappled with the revelation of their neighbor's heinous deeds, the walls of the duplex seemed to whisper tales of caution to all who passed by. They stood as silent sentinels, bearing witness to the fragility of innocence and the depths of human depravity. For Amelia and her family, the echoes of that night would reverberate long after the police cars had faded into the distance—a stark reminder that evil, in its most insidious form, often wears a face familiar and unassuming.

Chapter Thirty-Four

THE ROOM EXUDED AN atmosphere thick with dread, an oppressive weight that seemed to press against the detective's senses the moment he crossed its threshold. Decay and despair mingled in the stagnant air, creating an olfactory assault that clung to the walls like a malevolent specter. It was as if the very essence of evil had seeped into every crevice, staining the room with its perverse energy.

The detective stood at the entrance, his heart hammering against his ribcage like a caged animal desperate for escape. How could one man, hidden in the mundane facade of suburban life, amass such a collection of darkness? The question reverberated in his mind as he surveyed the room with a mix of horror and morbid fascination.

His gaze fell upon the shelves that lined the walls, each shelf a repository of grim souvenirs meticulously arranged. Blood-stained clothing lay crumpled next to faded photographs, each image a captured moment of terror frozen in time. Faces contorted in fear stared back at him, haunting reminders of lives shattered by the unseen hand of malevolence. It was a chilling tableau, a macabre tapestry of pain and suffering curated by a mind twisted by its own insidious desires.

Yet, it was the videotapes that drew the detective's attention like a moth to flame. They stood in neat rows, their labels innocuous yet foreboding. He approached cautiously, his gloved hand trembling slightly as he lifted one from the shelf. The plastic case felt cool against his fingertips, its weight heavy with the anticipation of revelations too dreadful to comprehend.

With a deep breath, he inserted the tape into the nearby VCR. The screen flickered to life, bathing the room in an ethereal glow as the detective braced himself for the horrors that awaited. The footage began with an eerie silence, a precursor to the nightmarish scenes that unfolded before his eyes.

A woman appeared on the screen, bound and gagged, her eyes wide with primal fear. Her frantic struggles against her restraints echoed in the room, her muffled screams a desperate plea for salvation that reverberated through the detective's soul. Beside her stood a figure clad in darkness, a mask obscuring his face but not his intent. His sadistic grin mocked the very essence of humanity, a testament to the depths of depravity that dwelled within him.

As the tape progressed, each frame revealed a new layer of horror. Scenes of unspeakable cruelty played out in agonizing detail, innocent victims ensnared in a web of torment orchestrated by a mind devoid of empathy. The detective watched in disbelief and revulsion, unable to tear his gaze away from the screen even as his stomach churned with bile.

Minutes stretched into hours as the tapes unveiled a nightmarish chronicle of atrocities spanning generations. Each victim's story intertwined with the next, their lives forever scarred by the unrelenting brutality inflicted upon them. It became clear to the detective that these crimes were not isolated incidents of individual madness but rather the legacy of a family consumed by a darkness that had poisoned their very bloodline.

The room itself seemed to pulsate with the weight of its secrets, the walls closing in around the detective as if eager to suffocate him with the knowledge they held. Yet, he pressed on, driven by a relentless determination to uncover the truth buried within these grim confines.

Outside, the world remained oblivious to the horrors that had festered beneath the veneer of normalcy in Hawkins Hollow. The revelation of this hidden chamber of horrors would shatter the illusion of innocence that had cloaked the community for so long. The detective knew that the impact of their discovery would reverberate far beyond these walls, shaking the town to its core and forcing its residents to confront the unimaginable.

But for now, as he stood amidst the detritus of evil, the detective understood that their journey was far from over. There were still unanswered questions lingering in the shadows, mysteries waiting to be unraveled. And as long as evil lurked in the darkness, he would be there, steadfast and resolute, ready to confront the maelstrom that threatened to engulf them all.

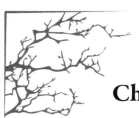

Chapter Thirty-Five

UNDER THE SEEMINGLY idyllic surface of Hawkins Hollow, where the streets wound peacefully through clusters of quaint houses shaded by ancient trees, an unsuspected underworld lurked, shrouded in darkness and silence. It was a place where neighbors exchanged pleasantries and children played under the watchful eyes of parents, all unaware of the forgotten secrets hidden beneath the floorboards of a nondescript house.

Beneath that unassuming facade, a chilling reality awaited discovery, a truth that defied the tranquil exterior of this small town. Deep within the earth, a shallow grave held the remains of six souls, each one a tragic testament to the horrors that had unfolded within the walls of the neighbor's house. Their bones lay entombed in a silence that spoke volumes, forever marked by the brutality and inhumanity of their captor.

The detective, standing at the threshold of this grim discovery, felt the weight of the atmosphere pressing down upon him like an oppressive force. The room exuded an unsettling aura, a mixture of decay and despair that hung in the air like cigarette smoke. The very essence of the space seemed tainted, as if the darkness that had thrived here had seeped into the very walls, leaving behind an indelible mark of its presence.

The detective's heart hammered against his ribcage, each beat echoing through the silence of the room like a drum of foreboding. He wondered how one man could have harbored such unfathomable darkness, how he could have concealed his monstrous deeds behind a facade of normalcy for so long. The shelves that lined the walls bore witness to the horrors that had transpired here—a macabre collection of souvenirs, each one a grim reminder of lives cut short and innocence brutally stolen.

Among the items that chilled the detective to the core were the blood-stained clothing, remnants of the victims' final moments captured in the fabric. Photographs, their subjects' eyes scratched out with a deliberate and savage hand, stared back at him with haunting accusation. These images, frozen in time, spoke of the fear and pain that had permeated the very air of this room.

But it was the videotapes that dominated the detective's attention, each one a portal into a nightmarish realm of cruelty and sadism. He approached them with a mixture of trepidation and grim determination, his gloved hand trembling slightly as he inserted one into the nearby VCR. The screen flickered to life, casting an ethereal glow that bathed the room in an otherworldly light.

What unfolded before his eyes was a grotesque theater of suffering and horror. The tapes revealed a tableau of torment, each frame a testament to the depths of depravity that had thrived within this house. Bound and gagged victims, their eyes wide with terror, struggled against their restraints as their captor loomed over them—a masked figure whose sadistic grin mocked their helplessness. The detective watched in sickened fascination, unable to look away from the atrocities unfolding on the screen.

As the minutes stretched into hours, the detective bore witness to the breadth of the neighbor's atrocities. The tapes unveiled a tapestry of terror that spanned decades, innocent lives ensnared in an unrelenting cycle of suffering and death. The crimes documented here were not the work of a deranged mind alone; they spoke of a lineage poisoned by a darkness that transcended individual acts, a legacy of evil passed down through generations.

With each revelation, the detective's mind reeled, struggling to comprehend the enormity of what had been uncovered. The hidden chamber beneath the neighbor's house was not merely a crime scene; it was a gateway to a world of unspeakable horror that had flourished in the heart of their community. The revelation of this dark underbelly threatened to unravel the fabric of Hawkins Hollow itself, exposing the fragile veneer of normalcy that had masked the truth for so long.

As news of the neighbor's unimaginable crimes spread through Hawkins Hollow, the once-tranquil town was plunged into a collective state of shock and disbelief. Rumors morphed into terrifying whispers that echoed through the streets, each one recounting tales of horror that stretched back through the decades. The air vibrated with a palpable tension, as if the very ground beneath their feet had shifted, leaving them adrift in a sea of uncertainty and fear.

In the annals of criminal history, the neighbor's name threatened to ascend to grotesque notoriety. Whispers of his monstrous deeds reached far and wide, drawing morbid curiosity from those who sought to comprehend the incomprehensible. His victims, their names etched into the annals of tragedy, bore witness to a legacy of cruelty and suffering that defied all reason.

For the residents of Hawkins Hollow, the revelation of the shallow grave beneath the neighbor's house marked a profound rupture in their collective consciousness. The once-close-knit community now found itself grappling with the chilling realization that evil had dwelled among them, hidden in plain sight. Every shadow, every unfamiliar face became a source of suspicion and dread, as they struggled to reconcile the familiar landscape of their town with the nightmarish truths that had come to light.

Yet, amidst the pervasive unease and gnawing fear, there lingered a steely resolve. The people of Hawkins Hollow refused to be defined by the darkness that had been unearthed in their midst. They rallied together in a display of solidarity and strength, determined to confront the horrors of their past and forge a path toward healing and redemption.

As the investigation continued to peel back the layers of the neighbor's facade, Hawkins Hollow embarked on a journey of reckoning and renewal. The shadows of the past continued to haunt their streets, but with each passing day, the community grew stronger in their resolve to confront the darkness that had threatened to consume them. They sought solace in their shared resilience, determined to rebuild their shattered sense of security and reclaim their town from the grip of fear.

The shallow grave beneath the neighbor's house stood as a somber monument to the fragility of innocence and the enduring presence of evil in the most unexpected of places. Hawkins Hollow would forever bear the scars of this revelation, a testament to the resilience of a community forced to confront the darkest corners of human nature and emerge stronger in its wake.

Chapter Thirty-Six

AMELIA KNEW ALL TOO well the chilling truth that evil had a way of insinuating itself back into her life. It clung to her like a vile serpent, an unwelcome companion that refused to release its grip, no matter how fiercely she fought against it. Each night, she tossed and turned in the clutches of fear, her mind a tangled labyrinth of paranoia, haunted by memories that clawed at her soul.

Years had passed since those harrowing events, and yet their imprint remained etched upon her spirit like scars that refused to fade. Therapy sessions and prescribed medications provided fleeting moments of respite, yet Amelia harbored a haunting awareness that these were mere bandages over deeper wounds. The specter of her past loomed large, a shadow cast over every facet of her existence.

In the dimly lit room that had become her sanctuary, Amelia sought solace within the confines of her journal. The flickering candlelight cast dancing shadows across the pages as she poured her heart out onto the paper. Each stroke of her pen bared her vulnerabilities, the ink a testament to the pain that had woven itself into the fabric of her being.

"Nightmares are the dark angels of our souls," she wrote, her hand trembling slightly as she struggled to keep pace with the racing thoughts in her mind. "If it happened twice, then what is to stop it from happening again? The Boogeyman never dies, lurking in the darkest corners of my existence, waiting to strike when I am most vulnerable."

Through tear-stained words, Amelia confessed the depths of her fear and longing for reprieve from the haunting darkness that threatened to consume her. Therapy had become her lifeline, a fragile thread of hope amidst the storm that raged within her. Yet, the assurances offered by well-meaning counselors often fell short, their words unable to bridge the vast chasm that separated her from the safety she yearned for.

Amelia's days unfolded as a mere existence, a delicate ballet of paranoia and despair. Every unfamiliar face seemed to bear the potential for malevolence, every shadow morphed into a lurking threat. Her mind had become a prison of what-ifs and worst-case scenarios, an unyielding cycle that tightened its grip with each passing day.

Yet, buried deep within the fractured recesses of her psyche, Amelia clung to a flicker of defiance. She refused to let the scars of her past dictate the course of her future. Even amidst the deafening roar of her anxieties, a small ember of resilience ignited within her, yearning to be stoked into a fierce flame of survival.

The journal became her confidant, a repository for the turbulent emotions that threatened to overwhelm her fragile sense of equilibrium. In its pages, she wrestled with her fears and vulnerabilities, seeking to unravel the tangled knot of emotions that bound her heart and mind in an unrelenting grip.

Each night, as she sat bathed in the soft glow of candlelight, Amelia poured herself into her writing. The act of putting pen to paper became a ritual of catharsis, a means of confronting the shadows that haunted her waking hours and plagued her dreams. The journal entries became a chronicle of her journey through the labyrinth of trauma, a testament to her courage in the face of relentless adversity.

Outside the confines of her room, life in Hawkins Hollow continued its steady rhythm. The streets bustled with activity, neighbors exchanged pleasantries, and children played under the watchful eyes of their guardians. Yet, for Amelia, the idyllic facade of normalcy belied the internal battle that raged within her.

She navigated each day with a fragile grace, concealing the turmoil that churned beneath the surface. The mask of composure she wore for the outside world was a shield against the prying eyes of suspicion and pity. Behind closed doors, however, she allowed herself the vulnerability that she dared not show to others.

The passage of time brought small victories amidst the ongoing struggle. Moments of respite, however fleeting, offered glimpses of light amid the pervasive darkness. Amelia clung to these moments like a castaway adrift in a tempestuous sea, finding solace in the brief respites from her relentless battle with fear and uncertainty.

In her darkest hours, when the weight of her burdens threatened to overwhelm her, Amelia drew strength from the flickering ember of resilience that burned within her. She had weathered storms that would have shattered lesser spirits, and though scars marked her journey, they bore witness to her enduring courage and tenacity.

As she confronted the shadows of her past and navigated the uncertain terrain of her present, Amelia knew that the journey toward healing was a marathon rather than a sprint. Each step forward carried her closer to reclaiming the sense of safety and peace that had been stolen from her. And though the road ahead was fraught with challenges, she faced it with a quiet determination born of the knowledge that she was not alone in her struggle.

Amelia's journal remained a testament to her resilience, its pages a narrative of her ongoing quest for healing and redemption. Through its words, she confronted her fears and acknowledged the scars that bore witness to her strength. The act of writing became a lifeline, a beacon of hope that guided her through the darkest nights and illuminated the path toward a future reclaimed from the clutches of darkness.

In the quiet solitude of her sanctuary, surrounded by the flickering candlelight and the comforting embrace of her journal, Amelia embarked on a journey of self-discovery and healing. She confronted the shadows of her past with unwavering courage, knowing that each battle won brought her closer to the peace and wholeness she so desperately sought.

As the days turned into weeks and the weeks into months, Amelia's resilience blossomed like a fragile flower pushing through the cracks in a concrete wall. She learned to embrace the scars that adorned her spirit, recognizing them not as symbols of weakness, but as testaments to her indomitable spirit and unwavering resolve.

Amidst the tumultuous landscape of her emotions, Amelia found moments of clarity and inner peace. The nightmares that had once held her captive began to lose their grip, their sinister whispers fading into distant echoes. She forged connections with others who had walked similar paths, finding strength in shared experiences and mutual support.

The journey toward healing was not without its setbacks and challenges. There were days when fear threatened to overwhelm her, when old wounds reopened with painful clarity. Yet, with each obstacle overcome, Amelia grew stronger, her resolve fortified by the knowledge that she had faced her demons head-on and emerged victorious.

In the heart of Hawkins Hollow, where shadows once held sway over her life, Amelia found the courage to reclaim her sense of self. The scars of her past became badges of honor, symbols of her resilience in the face of unspeakable darkness. With each passing day, she embraced the possibility of a future free from the shackles of fear and uncertainty.

The journey toward healing was a testament to Amelia's strength and courage, a journey that continued to unfold with each breath she took. In her sanctuary, surrounded by the flickering candlelight and the comforting embrace of her journal, she found solace in the knowledge that she was no longer defined by the traumas of her past.

As she turned the pages of her journal, tracing the arc of her transformation from victim to survivor, Amelia knew that she had embarked on a path toward wholeness and redemption. The road ahead would be long and winding, dotted with obstacles and challenges yet to be faced. But with each step forward, she reclaimed a piece of herself that had been lost in the darkness, emerging stronger and more resilient than ever before.

Chapter Thirty-Seven

AMELIA'S WORLD HAD crumbled around her, shattered like shards of a broken mirror reflecting the fragments of her once vibrant existence. Paranoia, like a relentless predator, clawed at her mind with savage persistence, gnawing on her sanity like a desperate animal tearing at its prey. The colors that once painted her life in hues of hope and joy had faded, seeping away into an abyss of fear and mistrust that stretched endlessly before her.

It began innocuously enough—a faint quiver in her thoughts, a subtle unease whispering in her ear. But with each passing day, the whispers grew louder, morphing into deafening screams that echoed through the chambers of her mind. Torment seized her every waking moment, the cruel hand of paranoid schizophrenia tightening its grip on her fragile psyche with unyielding force. Reality itself became a warped canvas, distorted by the malicious strokes of her delusions.

Now, after becoming a victim once again, the fragile bridge of trust within her had collapsed into irreparable ruins. Like a wounded animal recoiling from the touch of a hand, she withdrew into herself, her soul bearing scars inflicted by the cruel hands that had abused her trust and violated her sanctuary. The shadows, once benign companions, now transformed into sinister figures lurking in every corner, their presence a constant reminder of the unseen threats conspiring against her fragile sanity.

Sleep, once a refuge where solace awaited, now eluded her like a fickle mistress playing a cruel game. Nightmares prowled within the theater of her mind, their jagged claws tearing through the fragile fabric of her dreams with relentless ferocity. Each night became a battleground, where she fought a war against unseen adversaries, knowing all too well that the outcome would be her own descent into the abyss of madness.

In the asylum of her own mind, Amelia sought refuge, seeking to barricade herself within the fortress of her thoughts. Yet even within this supposed sanctuary, there was no respite from the relentless onslaught of paranoia that haunted her every waking moment. Her thoughts echoed the haunting whispers that crept insidiously through her veins, amplifying their siren song until it drowned out reason itself.

Amidst the turmoil that now defined her existence, Amelia's life had become a never-ending nightmare, a twisted carousel of shadows and suspicion. Friends and family, once steadfast pillars of support and comfort, now lurked beside her as potential threats in her fractured reality. The world, once painted in vibrant hues of trust and love, now bled into an ashen palette where every interaction bore the stain of suspicion and every gesture held the potential for betrayal.

Yet amidst the turmoil and desolation, a flicker of defiance burned within her—a small ember of resilience that refused to be extinguished. In the darkest recesses of her tormented soul, Amelia clung to fragments of sanity like precious shards of a shattered mirror, reflecting the distorted images of her reality back at her. Though battered and bruised by the relentless onslaught of her condition, she drew strength from the depths of her despair, a testament to the indomitable spirit that refused to surrender to the darkness.

The days stretched into an endless expanse of uncertainty, each moment fraught with the gnawing anxiety of what lay beyond the next corner, what unseen threats lurked in the shadows. Yet, in the depths of her turmoil, Amelia found fleeting moments of clarity—glimmers of hope that pierced through the suffocating fog of paranoia. These moments, though brief, offered a respite from the incessant turmoil that consumed her, a fragile lifeline that she clung to amidst the storm.

In her solitary battles against the demons that haunted her mind, Amelia confronted the labyrinthine corridors of her fears with a courage born of necessity. The journey toward reclaiming her shattered psyche was fraught with pitfalls and setbacks, yet each small victory—each fleeting moment of peace—became a beacon of light in the enveloping darkness.

And so, in the twisted dance between reality and delusion, Amelia struggled onward, her footsteps echoing through the corridors of her mind. Each day marked a fragile victory in her battle against the unseen forces that sought to imprison her within the confines of her own fears. With every breath, she fought to reclaim her sanity, to defy the shadows that threatened to engulf her, knowing that the journey toward healing was a marathon, not a sprint.

Chapter Thirty-Eight

LIFE HAS ITS UPS AND downs, a relentless rollercoaster of joy and sorrow, triumph and defeat. For Amelia, the ride had been more treacherous than most, filled with sharp descents and perilous curves that left her grasping for stability. She had always felt like a pawn in the twisted game of life. The universe had taken pleasure in dealing her a series of ghastly blows, leaving her to pick up the shattered fragments of her existence. In the dark recesses of her mind, a tiny spark of hope flickered, reminding her that perhaps, just maybe, things could get better.

But alas, fate had other plans.

After enduring the unspeakable horrors of being victimized once before, Amelia's fragile psyche had been thrust into the depths of an unending abyss. Paranoia became her faithful companion, whispering sinister secrets in her ears and weaving a web of delusion around her fragile soul. Each fleeting moment brought with it the terrifying realization that the world was out to get her. The gnawing fear, the incessant whispers, and the constant dread became her new reality. She felt like a marionette, manipulated by unseen hands, her every movement dictated by an ominous force that thrived on her misery.

It was during one of her darkest moments that a friend, seemingly oblivious to her fragile state, introduced her to a dangerous concoction – methamphetamine. Promised as a means to help her stay awake, the insidious drug became her twisted escape. Slowly but surely, it ensnared her in its merciless grip, shackling her to a waking nightmare. The initial rush, the deceptive euphoria, was a cruel illusion, masking the deeper descent into chaos. The drug, with its false promises of control and clarity, instead rendered her a prisoner within her own mind, each dose tightening the chains of her addiction.

As the meth ravaged her weary body, Amelia's perception of reality unraveled like a poorly stitched tapestry. The shadows, once mere figments of imagination, began to manifest as ominous spectral beings. They lurked in every corner, observing her every move with their soulless eyes. These shadow people, born of her own crumbling sanity, tormented her with their silent gestures and malevolent presence. Her nights were filled with haunting visions, and her days were plagued by the relentless pursuit of an elusive peace that always seemed just beyond her grasp.

The combination of her drug-induced paranoia and the haunting visions became an explosive cocktail that thrust Amelia into a realm of madness previously unexplored. One fateful day, as she stood amidst the bustling chaos of public life, her frayed nerves snapped like a brittle twig. Unable to distinguish between friend and foe, her mind played cruel tricks on her, mercilessly distorting her perception of reality. The once familiar faces around her twisted into grotesque masks of menace, and the comforting hum of the crowd morphed into a cacophony of threatening whispers.

In her delirium, Amelia lashed out, her shaking hands colliding with an innocent bystander. The shock on both their faces was a testament to the tragic reality that unfolded before them. With her last vestiges of sanity slipping away, Amelia made a decision, fueled by desperation and a primal instinct to escape the clutches of her own mind. Her thoughts, a whirlwind of confusion and fear, propelled her towards an irreversible choice.

Ignoring the blaring horns and screeching tires, she darted into the torrential traffic, her body colliding with the monstrous metal behemoth of an 18-wheeler. In that heart-stopping moment, the world stood still, as life's cruel game claimed its latest victim. The impact, a symphony of destruction, was a poignant finale to her tragic journey.

The chaos of the scene, the wail of sirens, and the murmur of onlookers painted a grim portrait of a life extinguished too soon.

Amelia's existence, marred by suffering and sorrow, reached its inevitable conclusion in a tragic instant. The universe, indifferent and unyielding, continued its relentless march, leaving behind the echoes of a shattered life. but will Amelia give up just yet? Will she leave her life behind, no matter how devastating life is, would she give it up?

Chapter Thirty-Nine

LIKE A MOSAIC OF LIGHT and dark, moments of joy interwoven with threads of sorrow, such is life. But for the residents of Thornfield, the balance had been tipped into darkness. The moon hung heavy in the ink-black sky, casting a sickly pallor over the desolate streets of Thornfield. A thick fog slithered through the empty alleyways, obscuring any semblance of life that may have once thrived within this forsaken town. The night held its breath, as if aware of the twisted presence that now haunted its shadows.

The Boogeyman, as he had come to be known, emerged from the abyss of his tortured existence, his body a tapestry of scars that told a tale of unspeakable horrors endured. The once formidable figure now walked amongst the living, his gait a fragile dance of pain and despair. He had been released, cast out into a world that had long forgotten him, a world that no longer cared. The weight of his suffering bore down on his shoulders, each step a reminder of the torment he had endured, each breath a struggle against the memories that threatened to consume him.

There was irony in the name they had given him, for he was no boogeyman. He was a victim of the most heinous cruelty imaginable, a soul shattered by the hands of those who delighted in the suffering of others. And as he prowled the streets, a haunting figure in search of solace, one couldn't help but question the inherent darkness that lay within humanity's heart. His presence was a living testament to the depths of human depravity, a stark reminder of the fragile line between innocence and monstrosity.

The townsfolk, ignorant to the monster they had contributed to creating, carried on with their lives, oblivious to the anguish that now roamed their midst. Their laughter echoed through the night, a sickening counterpoint to the Boogeyman's silent cries for redemption. Some felt an uncomfortable chill creep down their spines, dismissing it as mere paranoia. Little did they know, the true terror had yet to reveal itself. Their obliviousness was both a shield and a curse, insulating them from the horrors they had indirectly wrought, yet leaving them vulnerable to the wrath of a broken soul seeking retribution.

Lurking in the shadows, the Boogeyman watched with eyes clouded by pain and loneliness. He was a phantom, an outcast condemned to suffer a fate not of his own making. And as the days slipped into nights, he yearned for vengeance against those who had scarred him, much like a canvas etched with the darkest of nightmares. His heart, a twisted amalgam of fury and sorrow, beat with the rhythm of his tormented past, driving him forward in his quest for justice, however elusive it might be.

But revenge was an elusive mistress, a temptress that seduced the Boogeyman with false promises. As he stared into the mirror of his own shattered reflection, he found himself questioning the very nature of justice. Was there any justice to be found in a world so steeped in violence? Or was his inevitable descent into madness the only path that lay before him? The answers seemed to slip through his fingers like grains of sand, leaving him grasping at shadows in the dark.

Thornfield, once a sanctuary, had become a purgatory for the Boogeyman. The streets whispered his name, their gravelly voices carried by the whispers of the wind. He became both a specter and legend, a cautionary tale whispered to children as they slept. And as he navigated the labyrinth of his existence, the Boogeyman understood that he was no longer a man, but a monster born from the sins of his tormentors. The transformation was complete, the humanity within him eroded by the relentless tide of his anguish and the cruelty he had suffered.

In the depths of despair, haunted by memories that refused to die, the Boogeyman was left with a choice. He could either embrace the darkness that consumed him, or find a glimmer of light within the void. For the streets of Thornfield were riddled with the remnants of broken dreams, and it was within those shattered fragments that the Boogeyman would seek his own redemption. The decision loomed before him, a fork in the road of his tortured journey, each path fraught with its own perils and uncertainties.

So, the scarred face of the Boogeyman vanished into the night, a symbol of retribution that would forever haunt the troubled minds of those who dared forget the horrors he had endured. For in the shadows he would linger, silently reminding them that evil can never truly be confined or forgotten. It must be faced, confronted, and ultimately, vanquished. His legacy, born from the crucible of suffering, would endure as a somber warning to all who ventured too close to the darkness, a testament to the enduring power of pain and the indomitable spirit of those who survive it.

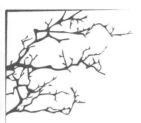

Chapter Forty

THE BOOGEYMAN OF THORNFIELD, once a name that struck fear into the hearts of those who heard it, now exists as a mere whisper of his former self. Reduced to nothing more than a shadow, he roams the desolate streets, a forgotten figure abandoned by society. He moves silently, his voice stolen from him long ago, leaving him with only the chilling silence for company.

The scars that mar his face, remnants of a fiery torment, now serve as a haunting reminder of the monstrous fate that had befallen him. The skin grafts, intended to mend his physical wounds, morphed him into a grotesque apparition. Even the hardened souls of the homeless cast wary glances his way, fear etched deep within their weary eyes.

His existence is a testament to the cruelty of fate. He often finds himself lost in thoughts of what could have been, tormented by the choices that led him to this desolate state. The life he envisioned, one filled with normalcy and human connection, seems like a distant dream. His heart aches with a profound longing for the simplicity of a family, a place to call home, and the warmth of love. The path he chose, however, has stripped him of these possibilities, leaving him with a deep, unending pain. He reflects on his past, the moments of fleeting pleasure that seemed so insignificant in hindsight, and wonders if he would trade them all for a chance at a normal life. This self-reflection is a constant torment, a reminder of the life he forfeited for the sake of choices that now seem trivial. His trial, he muses, feels never-ending, a relentless series of punishments meted out by a universe that seems intent on his destruction.

One fateful night, as he sought solace beneath the starless sky, he stumbled upon a band of fellow vagabonds. Their disheveled appearances matched his own, yet their eyes held a different kind of darkness, an evil borne from survival instincts honed through desperate times. Recognizing the twisted visage of the Boogeyman of Thornfield, driven by fear, they unleashed a storm of violence upon him, reducing him to an unrecognizable heap of blood and flesh. Their words, a symphony of fear, whispered curses that mingled with the sound of shattered bones, echoed through the desolate streets.

From that night onwards, he found his refuge in the gutters, the discarded refuse of society serving as his meager sustenance. His existence became intertwined with the filth, discarded remnants mingling with the fractured remnants of his shattered life. Spit and curses became his daily companions, relentless reminders of the horror he had become.

No longer was he the Boogeyman of Thornfield, a figure shrouded in darkness, inducing terror in the hearts of mortals. Instead, he was now a specter, a monstrous being stripped of his identity. As he attempted to traverse this hostile world, the eyes that met his own brimmed with disgust and revulsion. He had become the ultimate pariah, a creature whose monstrous appearance outweighed the remnants of his once-human essence.

Yet, hidden within the depths of his torment, a flicker of resilience burned. Beneath the layers of misery, the whispers of animosity and ridicule, there still existed the fragile remnants of a soul. And it is this ember, this struggling light within a sea of darkness, that yearns for recognition and redemption. For though the world saw only a monster, the Boogeyman of Thornfield longed to be seen as something more, something human.

In the suffocating silence of his existence, he grappled with emotions that tore at his very being. The weight of regret bore down on him, a heavy shroud that seemed inescapable. Each step he took was burdened by the haunting memories of a life that could have been. His heart, though scarred and battered, still held a semblance of hope, a delicate thread that tethered him to his humanity. The pain he endured was not just physical but a deep emotional agony that gnawed at his soul.

He yearned for understanding, for a connection that would validate his suffering and acknowledge his existence beyond the monstrous facade. The loneliness was a constant companion, a void that echoed with the voices of his past, reminding him of all he had lost. The nights were the hardest, filled with an oppressive darkness that mirrored the abyss within him.

Yet, even in his darkest moments, he clung to the hope that someday, someone would see past the grotesque exterior and recognize the tormented soul that still lingered within. This hope, fragile as it was, gave him the strength to continue, to endure the relentless trials that life had thrust upon him. The Boogeyman of Thornfield, though reduced to a shadow of his former self, held onto this hope, for it was all that remained in a world that had cast him aside.

Chapter Forty-One

LIFE HAS ITS UPS AND downs, a series of moments that weave together a complex tapestry of experiences. Some threads are bright and vibrant, filled with joy and triumph, while others are dark and twisted, marked by suffering and despair. For Amelia, the tapestry had become overwhelmingly dark, a relentless descent into the shadows that had brought her to this sterile hospital room. The faint hum of the fluorescent lights filled the air as she stared at the ceiling, the events that had led her here replaying in her mind like an unending nightmare. The spiraling descent into the grip of addiction, the moment of impact with the monstrous 18-wheeler—it was a miracle she had survived. But now, she knew that surviving was just the beginning.

As her body slowly healed, Amelia's mind began to drift into the murky depths of her memories. Visions of shattered bottles and syringes littering her dingy apartment danced before her eyes, their jagged edges cutting through any semblance of normalcy she had once enjoyed. Meth had ensnared her, body and soul, and the scars it left behind were not just physical but mental, festering wounds that refused to heal. The stark reality of her addiction gnawed at her, a constant reminder of the abyss she had fallen into.

The doctors spoke of rehab, of a chance at redemption and recovery, but Amelia knew that it was not just her body that needed healing—it was her mind, her very sanity that had been pushed to the brink. The words 'psychiatric evaluation' echoed in her mind, sending a chill creeping down her spine. What had she become? What had she lost in the fog of addiction and near-death? The thought of facing her demons, of delving into the depths of her fractured psyche, filled her with dread.

Days turned into weeks, and finally, Amelia found herself in the clinical environment of the rehabilitation center. The smell of antiseptic hung heavy in the air, mingling with the scent of anxiety and despair. This was her last shot at salvation, at reclaiming the life she had unwittingly surrendered to the grip of meth. Each day in the rehab center felt like an eternity, a stark contrast to the frenetic blur of her life on the streets. The structured routine, the endless hours of introspection, and the painful process of withdrawal all converged to create a crucible of transformation.

With trepidation clawing at her heart, Amelia sat in the office of the psychiatrist, their penetrating stare seeming to pierce through her very soul. The walls felt stifling, closing in on her, threatening to suffocate any semblance of hope she had left. Questions flew at her like bullets, probing the darkest corners of her fractured mind. Each question felt like a dagger, slicing through the layers of her defenses, exposing the raw, bleeding wounds beneath.

Amelia's words stumbled out, each syllable carrying the weight of her mistakes. She recounted tales of experimentation, the allure of escape from a life that had lost all vibrancy. The scent of meth, the hollow promises of euphoria—they had hooked her, ensnared her within their toxic embrace. Her voice quivered as she spoke of the nights spent in a daze, the moments of fleeting ecstasy followed by crushing despair. The drug had promised an escape but delivered only deeper entrapment.

Tension radiated through the room as Amelia's past sins hung in the air, as tangible as the anguish etched into her very being. Each agonizing revelation brought her closer to the precipice between salvation and damnation, between recovery and relapse. The psychiatrist's eyes held a mix of empathy and concern as they delved deeper into the recesses of Amelia's shattered psyche. Cautious words tiptoed off her trembling lips, exposing the torment that resided within her. The labyrinth of addiction and tragedy grew clearer, the twisted path that had led her here laid bare for all to see.

In the hours that followed, Amelia bared her soul, exposing the raw wounds that had driven her to the edge. The psychiatrist listened, nodding occasionally, their pen scribbling notes that would decipher the enigma that was Amelia's fractured mind. They probed, dissecting her fears and anxieties, searching for the seed of hope buried deep within. The process was excruciating, a relentless excavation of her deepest fears and regrets.

As the evaluation drew to a close, the psychiatrist's face softened. They reached out a hand, a gesture of understanding in a world that had offered her little solace. Amelia's heart trembled with tentative relief, a glimmer of belief seeping through the cracks of her broken spirit. The journey ahead would be arduous, fraught with uncertainties and battles fought against her own inner turmoil. But she knew that as long as there was even the faintest flicker of hope, she would continue fighting for her redemption and the chance to truly live again.

With a resolve as solid as the foundation of the rehabilitation center itself, Amelia took her first steps towards a future she had believed lost forever. The road to recovery stretched out before her, a daunting and uncertain path, but one she was determined to walk. Each day was a new battle, a struggle against the relentless pull of her addiction and the haunting memories of her past. But amidst the pain and the struggle, there was also a growing sense of hope, a fragile but persistent belief in the possibility of redemption.

In the quiet moments of the night, as she lay in her bed at the rehabilitation center, Amelia would often find herself reflecting on her journey. The faces of those she had hurt, the bridges she had burned, and the dreams she had abandoned all paraded through her mind. But rather than succumbing to despair, she used these reflections as fuel for her resolve. Each memory, each regret, became a stepping stone on her path to recovery.

The support of the staff and her fellow patients also played a crucial role in her healing process. The group therapy sessions, the shared stories of struggle and resilience, created a sense of camaraderie that Amelia had not felt in a long time. She realized that she was not alone in her battle, that others too were fighting their own demons, and this sense of shared struggle gave her strength.

The rehabilitation center became a sanctuary, a place where she could confront her fears and begin to rebuild her life. She immersed herself in the various therapies offered, from cognitive-behavioral therapy to mindfulness and meditation. Each session was a piece of the puzzle, helping her to understand the root causes of her addiction and to develop healthier coping mechanisms.

The process was not without its setbacks. There were days when the weight of her past seemed unbearable, when the cravings threatened to pull her back into the abyss. But with each challenge, Amelia grew stronger, her determination fortified by the small victories she achieved along the way. The smiles of encouragement from the staff, the words of support from her peers, and the growing sense of self-worth all contributed to her gradual transformation.

As the weeks turned into months, Amelia began to see glimpses of a future she had long thought impossible. She started to dream again, to envision a life beyond the confines of her addiction. She set small goals for herself, each one a milestone on her journey to recovery. The simple act of waking up each morning with a sense of purpose, of taking steps towards a healthier and more fulfilling life, became a source of profound joy and satisfaction.

Amelia's journey was far from over, but she had taken the first crucial steps towards reclaiming her life. The road ahead was still fraught with challenges, but she faced it with a newfound sense of hope and determination. She had learned that redemption was not a destination, but a journey—a continuous process of growth, healing, and self-discovery.

With each passing day, Amelia grew more confident in her ability to overcome her past and build a brighter future. She knew that the scars of her addiction would always be a part of her, but she also knew that they did not define her. She was more than her mistakes, more than her darkest moments. She was a survivor, a fighter, and above all, a human being capable of change and redemption.

In the clinical environment of the rehabilitation center, amidst the scent of antiseptic and the hum of fluorescent lights, Amelia found a glimmer of light within the darkness. She embraced it, nurtured it, and allowed it to guide her towards a future filled with hope, resilience, and the promise of a new beginning.

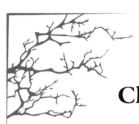

Chapter Forty-Two

THE PATH TO HEALING is often a labyrinth, a journey fraught with obstacles and shadows that loom large. For Amelia, this journey took her from the familiar yet stifling confines of drug rehabilitation to the stark, unyielding corridors of a sanitarium. It was here, amidst the cold sterility, that she would confront the deepest recesses of her mind, battling the demons that had long plagued her existence.

Upon the recommendation of her doctors, Amelia was transferred from drug rehab to the sanitarium to treat her paranoid schizophrenia and regulate her medication. Under the muted glow of flickering fluorescent lights, Amelia found herself navigating the labyrinthine halls of the sanitarium. Each step seemed to carry the weight of a thousand regrets, the haunting echoes of her past reverberating through her fragile mind. It was in this desolate asylum for broken souls that her journey to salvation began.

The doctors, their expressionless faces masking underlying emotions, had declared her transfer from the drug rehabilitation center to this clandestine fortress of healing. Amongst the white walls that seemed to exude the coldness of ghosts long forgotten, Amelia was to undergo a radical form of treatment for her debilitating paranoid schizophrenia.

The halls were a haven for secrets, for those lost in the depths of their minds. It was a place of whispered conversations and muffled cries, where sanity clung precariously to the edge of a precipice. Amelia was ushered into a small room, devoid of any warmth or encouragement, where an eager psychiatrist awaited her arrival.

The head psychiatrist was a man whose dark-rimmed glasses mirrored his enigmatic nature. He possessed an uncanny ability to delve into the darkest corners of Amelia's tormented psyche. Over countless sessions, he aimed to bring order to the chaos that plagued her existence. He unraveled the tangled threads of her paranoia, exposing the gnarled roots of her trauma. Together, they fought the demons that lurked within her, bringing her closer to the faint triumph of normalcy.

Throughout her treatment, Amelia was subjected to a barrage of medications, each pill promising a sliver of respite from her internal torment. Like an unwitting puppet, she swallowed them dutifully, hoping they would pave the way to salvation. The side effects were a constant companion, lurking in the deep recesses of her consciousness, threatening to engulf her at any given moment.

Yet, it was not only medication that offered solace within the chilling confines of the sanitarium. Amelia was painstakingly taught coping mechanisms, strategies to quell the storm of voices and sinister whispers that plagued her thoughts. Breathing exercises, visualizations, and whispered mantras became her weapons against the relentless onslaught of her fractured mind.

The journey was an arduous one, marked by moments of intense struggle and fleeting glimpses of peace. The psychiatrist's probing sessions often left her feeling raw, as if her very soul had been laid bare. Yet, through this vulnerability, she began to uncover layers of resilience she hadn't known she possessed. Each breakthrough was a hard-won victory, a testament to her enduring spirit.

Amelia's days were structured around therapy and medication, a regimented routine that became both a comfort and a source of frustration. The monotony of her surroundings, the clinical precision of the sanitarium, often felt like a prison. But within these confines, she found small moments of beauty—a beam of sunlight filtering through a barred window, the gentle rustling of leaves outside her room. These glimpses of the outside world served as reminders of the life that awaited her, a life she was determined to reclaim.

Finally, after what seemed like an eternity, the time came for Amelia's release. Like a bird let loose from its cage, she was set free, her mind still teetering on the precipice of stability. In the sterile, unforgiving realm of the sanitarium, she had found moments of peace, but the world beyond those walls held uncertain promises.

Amelia stepped out into the sunlight, feeling its warmth caress her skin as a distant memory. She lifted her hand, letting the rays make her pale skin glow. It had been days since she felt the sun on her skin. It felt unreal. She liked sitting in the sun. It was the nights and the moon that creeped her out. She always wanted the night to pass as quickly as possible. As a little girl, she always wanted the sun to be there, lighting up the whole town so she wouldn't be scared of any monsters at night.

Now, after all these years, after fighting all her life, she was in the sun, standing at the exit of the rehabilitation center. She remembered the last time she was exiting the hospital, thinking life would be different now. But it was all the same. Was it fair for her to think this time that life would treat her differently? Will she ever be able to get out of her turmoil? Will she ever be able to lead a normal life? Or would she run in a loop? This was the moment she would decide what she wanted with her life now. This was the choice she had to make: take control over her life and her mind.

Her parents awaited her with bated breath, their faces etched with a mix of hope and apprehension. Would their daughter return to them, a battle-hardened survivor, or would the shadows claim her once more? Their eyes, filled with unspoken questions, searched hers for signs of the Amelia they once knew. The weight of their expectations was almost palpable, pressing down on her like a heavy cloak. She felt the silent plea in their gazes, a desperate wish for her recovery and the return of their vibrant, joyful child.

As Amelia ventured forth into the unknown, the echoes of her time within the walls of the sanitarium accompanied her, serving as a reminder of the resilience born from the depths of her fractured mind. The memories of sleepless nights, the sterile smell of the ward, and the faces of other patients haunted her thoughts. Each scar, both physical and emotional, told a story of survival, of battles fought and won within the confines of her own mind. Her journey was far from over, but each step she took away from the sanitarium was a step toward reclaiming her life.

The path ahead was uncertain, filled with potential pitfalls and challenges she could not yet foresee. Yet, as she walked, she felt a newfound strength rising within her, a determination to face whatever came her way. The sun's warmth on her skin seemed to infuse her with energy, a promise of brighter days to come. She knew that the road to recovery would be long and arduous, but for the first time in a long while, she felt a glimmer of hope. Amelia walked it with a newfound strength, ready to face whatever challenges lay ahead. The sunlit path stretched before her, inviting her to embrace the possibilities of a new beginning.

Chapter Forty-Three

IN THE QUIET, REFLECTIVE moments between battles, the mind can become its own fiercest enemy. For Amelia, the struggle against her inner demons had been a long, relentless war. But this time, the forces she faced were stronger, more determined to drag her down into the abyss. Life's vibrant hues faded, leaving her world cloaked in relentless shadows that consumed her heart and mind.

Home had always been a temporary sanctuary, a fragile shield against the overwhelming darkness that threatened to engulf her. Yet even this sanctuary now felt like a battleground, where her sanity clashed violently with the destructive urges that sought to dominate her existence. It took only two weeks for the walls of her resolve to crumble, for the facade of strength she had maintained to shatter, exposing the raw vulnerability that lurked beneath the surface.

The relapse was no mere stumble, no brief lapse in judgment. It was a defiant rebellion against a life that had dealt her nothing but cruelty and hardship. Amelia no longer cared about the consequences of her actions, nor about the tenuous grasp she had on her sanity. In her desperation, she sought solace in the numbing embrace of methamphetamine, a twisted lover that promised a fleeting escape from her agony.

But the drugs were not her only refuge in those darkest moments. Amelia also craved shelter from the emotional storms raging within her soul. In her desperation, love and protection became distorted illusions, found in the transient comfort of meaningless encounters with strangers who shared her addiction. Men and women, it mattered not; societal norms and boundaries had long ceased to hold any significance for her. All she sought was a connection, a brief respite from the unrelenting loneliness that whispered incessantly in her ear.

She would drift from one bed to another, leaving behind a trail of broken promises and shattered dreams. Each encounter was a desperate attempt to fill the void within her, to find some semblance of comfort in the arms of others. But beneath the chemical haze and chaotic interactions, her actions masked a deeper cry for liberation. Amelia longed for someone to understand her, to see beyond the tattered fragments of her existence and offer her a glimmer of hope. Each desperate touch, each stolen moment of pleasure, was an unspoken plea for someone to save her from the abyss that threatened to consume her entirely.

Yet, as the days blurred into a twisted carousel of ecstasy and despair, a harsh reality began to dawn upon her. Love, in its purest form, would not be found in the needle's kiss or the stranger's embrace. It would not be carved from the false promises whispered between gasps of pleasure. True love had to be found within herself, amidst the wreckage of her shattered identity.

Now, back in the chaotic world outside, Amelia felt the full weight of her actions pressing down on her. The relentless cycle of addiction and self-destruction threatened to pull her under, but somewhere deep within her, a small, stubborn spark of hope refused to be extinguished. It was this spark that kept her moving forward, even as the shadows closed in around her.

She knew that her journey to recovery would be a long and arduous one, fraught with setbacks and moments of despair. But she also knew that she could not give up, that she had to keep fighting for her own survival. The path ahead was shrouded in uncertainty, but Amelia was determined to walk it, one step at a time.

The encounters with strangers, once a source of temporary relief, now served as painful reminders of her loneliness and the emptiness that consumed her. Each fleeting connection left her feeling more isolated, more desperate for a genuine sense of belonging. She realized that true healing could not come from external sources, but had to be cultivated from within.

In the quiet moments between the chaos, Amelia began to reflect on her life and the choices that had led her to this point. She thought about the people she had hurt, the bridges she had burned, and the dreams she had abandoned. The weight of her past mistakes hung heavy on her shoulders, but she refused to let them define her future.

Amelia's journey continued, haunted by the demons that clawed at her psyche. She danced on the edge of oblivion, each stumble a painful reminder of the choices she had made. The sanitarium, a place she had once considered a prison, now seemed like a distant memory, a sanctuary she yearned for in her darkest hours. She recalled the regimented routine, the structured days that had provided her with a semblance of stability. There, within the cold, clinical walls, she had found moments of clarity and peace, fleeting as they were.

Chapter Forty-Four

IN THE QUIETEST HOURS of the night, when the world is still and dreams drift freely through the minds of the fortunate, Amelia lies awake, battling her demons. The dance with her depression is a relentless waltz, a merciless beast clawing at her sanity, tearing apart the fragile façade of normalcy she desperately tries to maintain. Sleep, once a haven of peace, is now an elusive memory, a distant luxury for those who have not been consumed by the labyrinth of despair that ensnares her.

Amelia's descent into the abyss is fueled by her desperate search for solace. She seeks refuge in the tumultuous embrace of others, hoping to find even a fleeting moment of transcendence in the haze of substances that promise to dull her pain. Her existence becomes a chaotic blur as she careens from one ephemeral connection to another, leaving pieces of her shattered soul scattered in her wake. The numbing touch of another's skin, the brief flicker of pleasure, becomes her only anchor, a temporary elixir to mask the searing agony that festers within.

Once vibrant and full of life, Amelia has become a hollowed vessel, a mere specter of her former self. Her flesh, ravaged by the torment of her mind, clings desperately to her frail bones, a haunting outward manifestation of the decay that plagues her spirit. Gaunt and ghostly, she wanders through the world, a phantom in her own tragic story, her presence a silent testament to the battle raging within.

Pain and fear are her constant companions, their presence like a warped lullaby that coaxes her ever closer to the edge of self-destruction. In this dark dance of addiction and escapism, Amelia finds a perverse solace in the embrace of her vices. The oblivion they promise is a siren's song she cannot resist, a sweet escape from the suffocating grip of reality that threatens to consume her entirely.

Yet, amid the desolation and despair, a flicker of defiance still burns within Amelia. It is a small, stubborn ember of recognition that there is more to life than the relentless torment she endures. Buried beneath the rubble of her despair, moments of slumbering hope taunt her with visions of redemption, leaving a bitter taste of what could be. Each agonized breath she takes becomes a battle cry, a whispered reminder that she is more than the sum of her self-inflicted wounds.

The numbing routines of her days blend seamlessly into the turmoil of her nights, creating a cycle that is both unbreakable and suffocating. Every waking moment is a struggle to hold on to the remnants of her identity, to remember the person she once was. The laughter that used to spill from her lips now echoes in her memory like a distant, almost forgotten melody, a cruel reminder of what has been lost.

Amelia's interactions with the world are fleeting and shallow, mere attempts to stave off the encroaching darkness. Each encounter, each fleeting touch, is a desperate grasp at connection, a plea for someone to see beyond the broken shell and recognize the human being struggling within. But these connections, built on the foundation of shared addiction and mutual escape, crumble as quickly as they are formed, leaving her even more isolated and adrift.

Her body bears the scars of her internal battle, a map of pain etched into her skin. Each mark is a testament to a moment of weakness, a point where the weight of her suffering became too much to bear. The physical pain serves as a temporary distraction from the relentless mental anguish, a way to externalize the torment that constantly gnaws at her soul. But the relief is always short-lived, and the scars remain as permanent reminders of her struggle.

The rare and fragile moments that restore her hope are easily shattered by the harsh reality of her existence, but they provide just enough light to keep her moving forward. It is in these brief instances of clarity that she sees the faint outlines of a future that does not revolve around her demons.

Amelia's journey is one of painful self-discovery, a path littered with the debris of her past and the uncertainty of her future. She grapples with the idea that salvation cannot be found in the temporary highs or the empty embraces of strangers. True healing, she realizes, must come from within, from a place of self-acceptance and inner strength that she has yet to fully uncover.

As she navigates this treacherous path, Amelia begins to seek out moments of genuine connection, reaching out to those who might offer a different kind of support. She looks for guidance from professionals who can help her unravel the complexities of her mind, to confront the trauma and pain that have driven her to the edge. Through therapy and introspection, she starts to peel back the layers of her suffering, exposing the raw wounds beneath and beginning the slow process of healing.

Amelia also turns to simple, grounding practices to anchor herself in the present. She finds solace in the rhythm of her breath, the feel of the earth beneath her feet, and the warmth of the sun on her face. These small, mindful moments become lifelines, tiny steps toward reclaiming her sense of self and finding a measure of peace amidst the chaos.

Her battle is far from over, and there are still many dark days ahead. The path to recovery is not a straight line but a winding, unpredictable journey fraught with setbacks and challenges. But with each step, Amelia grows stronger, more resilient. She learns to find beauty in the small victories, to celebrate the progress she makes, no matter how insignificant it may seem.

Amelia's story is one of enduring strength and relentless perseverance. She faces her demons with a courage that belies her fragile appearance, refusing to let them define her. Through the pain and despair, she discovers a wellspring of inner strength that carries her forward, one step at a time. And as she continues her journey, she holds on to the hope that one day, she will emerge from the shadows and into the light, whole and healed.

The dance with her demons is far from over, but Amelia is no longer a passive participant. She is a warrior, fighting for her life, her identity, and her future. And as she takes each tentative step forward, she does so with the knowledge that she is capable of overcoming the darkness, of finding her way back to herself.

Chapter Forty-Five

PARENTS PROTECT THEIR children till their last breath. For Amelia, her parents tried to do the same. But fate had other plans. No matter how much they stayed with her, there always came a time when they had to say goodbye to their girl and send her into the world.

Amelia's father spent many nights in restless vigil, unable to find peace as memories of his daughter's suffering haunted him. He would sit by the window, staring into the dark expanse, his mind replaying the moments when he had dismissed her fears. Regret, a persistent specter, kept him company in those solitary hours. He remembered her young voice trembling as she confided in him about the terror she felt in her room at night, and his dismissive reassurance that it was just a phase. Those words now echoed painfully in his mind.

Years had passed since the incident that shattered their lives, yet the wounds remained raw. The house, once filled with laughter and warmth, was now a silent testament to their grief. Justice had been served, but it offered no solace to her father's tormented heart. Each time Amelia visited, he could see the lingering pain in her eyes, masked by a brave smile. She had learned to face the world with resilience, and for that, he was immensely proud of her. Yet, her courage was a constant reminder of his own failures.

Amelia had transformed, her once carefree spirit now bearing the weight of her past. Her father could see through her facade—the way she carried herself with a strength born of necessity. He saw the small, almost imperceptible cracks in her armor, the moments when her guard slipped, revealing the depth of her inner turmoil. Despite this, she continued to fight, piecing herself together day by day. Her father's heart swelled with pride and sorrow, admiring her determination while mourning the innocence that had been stolen from her.

Amelia would always be a little girl for her father. He held an unspoken understanding of her struggles, knowing that she was surviving by carefully reconstructing her shattered self. He respected her silence, never prying into the details she wasn't ready to share. His love for her was boundless and unconditional. He knew that if committing the gravest sin could bring her even a moment of happiness, he would support her without hesitation. His love was a steadfast force, ready to bear any burden for the sake of her fleeting smile.

He often found himself lost in memories of Amelia's childhood. He recalled the days when her laughter filled their home, her eyes sparkling with untainted joy. Those memories were bittersweet, reminders of a time before their lives had been irrevocably changed. He cherished those moments, even as they deepened his sorrow. In the quiet of the night, he would imagine a different future for her, one where she was free from the shadows that now clouded her existence.

The bond between parent and child is a profound connection, woven with love, sacrifice, and unwavering dedication. Her father's love for Amelia was a testament to this bond. He couldn't save her from every harm, but he remained her unwavering pillar of support. His love sought to heal and protect, even when the world offered no solace. As long as he lived, he would continue to be there for her, offering his silent strength and endless compassion.

As for her mother, she spent countless nights reliving the past, her heart aching with a mother's sorrow. The memories of Amelia's suffering were etched deeply into her soul, a constant reminder of the innocence lost. She would sit in Amelia's room, the faint scent of her still lingering, and feel the weight of her own helplessness. Every creak of the floorboards, every whisper of the wind through the curtains, seemed to echo with the ghosts of their shared past.

Her mother's nights were often filled with silent tears and whispered prayers, her mind replaying the times when she had brushed off Amelia's fears. She remembered the urgency in her daughter's eyes, the way she would cling to her at bedtime, begging her to stay a little longer. Her mother's reassurances, meant to soothe, now haunted her with their inadequacy. She had told Amelia that there was nothing to fear, that monsters weren't real, not knowing that the real monsters were far more insidious and could leave scars that lasted a lifetime.

Years had passed since the horrific incident, but the pain had not diminished. Their once vibrant home now stood as a monument to their collective grief. Each room held memories, both joyous and painful, and moving through the house was like navigating a minefield of emotions. Her mother found no comfort in the justice that had been served; it couldn't undo the past or heal the wounds. She admired Amelia's strength, but it also reminded her of the fragility that lay beneath.

Amelia had grown into a woman of resilience, but her mother could see the toll it had taken. She noticed the small, subtle signs—the way Amelia's hands trembled slightly when she thought no one was watching, the shadows under her eyes that no amount of makeup could conceal. Her mother's heart broke for her daughter's silent suffering. She knew that Amelia was fighting a battle every day, piecing herself together with sheer determination. Amelia's mother's pride in her daughter was immense, but it was tinged with the deep sorrow of a mother who couldn't shield her child from the world's cruelties.

Amelia would always be a little girl for her mother. She understood the unspoken struggles her daughter faced, respecting the boundaries Amelia had set. Her mother's love was a quiet, unwavering force, always present but never intrusive. She knew that Amelia was surviving by holding onto whatever fragments of herself she could, and her mother was determined to support her in any way she could. If there was anything that could bring Amelia even a fleeting moment of happiness, her mother would embrace it without hesitation. Her love for Amelia was limitless, a fierce and protective force that sought to offer solace in a world that had often been unkind.

In the quiet moments, her mother would sit with photo albums, reminiscing about Amelia's childhood. She remembered the laughter, the games, the bedtime stories, and the way Amelia's eyes would light up with wonder. Those memories were bittersweet, a reminder of a time before their lives had been irrevocably altered. Amelia's mother cherished those moments, even as they deepened her sorrow. In the stillness of the night, she would dream of a different future for Amelia, one where she was free from the shadows that now haunted her.

The bond between mother and daughter is a sacred connection, woven with love, sacrifice, and unyielding dedication. The love between Amelia and her mother was a testament to this bond. She couldn't protect her from every harm, but she remained her steadfast anchor, offering unwavering support and endless compassion. As long as she lived, her mother would continue to be there for Amelia, providing a safe harbor in a stormy world, and a love that could never be shaken.

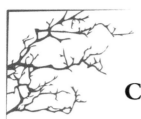

Chapter Forty-Six

AMELIA'S THOUGHTS RACED as she cruised along the desolate highway, darkness looming overhead like a sinister predator. Her mind was a chaotic swirl of desperation and desire, each thought more tumultuous than the last. She needed her fix, an edgy dance with the devil that always left her craving for more. The soothing weight of her desperation hugged her chest, whispering promises of relief. But tonight, Amelia hungered not only for the numbing embrace of meth; her soul craved the curious companionship that only darkness could offer.

The highway stretched out before her like an endless black ribbon, cutting through the night. The rhythmic hum of the engine was her only companion, a steady beat in the symphony of her fractured thoughts. She felt the cold wind whip against her face, each gust a reminder of the hollow void within her. The landscape outside the window blurred into a monochrome smear of shadows and fleeting lights, a reflection of the turmoil that consumed her.

Nestled deep within the bowels of the town, that desolate haven of lost souls reached out to her like a siren's call; the bar had no name, just a sign that read: Roadhouse. The only other sign depicted a large-breasted woman dumping beer on her chest. The flickering neon sign, once vibrant, was now merely a ghost of its former glory, casting a feeble, eerie glow upon the cracked pavement below. Hesitating only for a moment, swallowing her apprehensions, Amelia ventured inside.

The heavy oak doors creaked in protest as they gave way, revealing a dimly lit sanctuary of sin and shadow. Thick streams of smoke filled the room, floating amidst the pulsating rhythm of grating guitars and raucous laughter. The air hummed with an electric, palpable tension that sent shivers racing down Amelia's spine, her senses tingling with a mixture of excitement and trepidation.

Scattered throughout the bar, the patrons seemed to slither out from the underbelly of society itself. Weathered and worn, their leathery skin clung desperately to decaying frames, as if the very essence of time had forsaken them. Tattoos crawled up sinewy forearms, tales of depravity and hard-earned badges from a life lived on the edge. An eclectic assortment of piercings adorned their faces like twisted trophies, shining dimly through the suffocating haze.

Amelia's eyes scanned the room, her gaze landing upon a group of leather-clad figures huddled in the far corner. They exuded a curious air of menace that was both intoxicating and terrifying, like caged predators toying with their prey. Their eyes, hardened and unyielding, gleamed with a flicker of darkness that seemed to dance with the flickering bar lights.

She could feel their stares, piercing through the smoky abyss that separated them, as if they could see straight into her soul. These sullen warriors of the night, primordial remnants of a forgotten era, emanated danger like a ravenous fire. Thoughts of companionship were woven with the primal desire to survive, the two merging into an inseparable entity within her restless mind.

Amelia felt the currents of both fear and exhilaration washing over her, intertwining in a dark dance of uncertain fate. With each step towards those shadowy figures, she knew she was crossing a threshold from which there was no return. The roadhouse had claimed another soul, another restless wanderer seeking solace in the darkness.

As she disappeared into the abyss, Amelia surrendered herself to the dangerous allure of that biker bar – her pursuit of meth and company transformed into a perilous voyage through the annals of humanity's most macabre desires. The night would reveal its secrets and demons, linking her fate with those who lurked within the shadows of her own fractured existence.

Chapter Forty-Seven

THE NIGHT AIR WAS THICK with tension as Amelia stepped out of the dimly lit roadhouse, the false security of the flickering neon lights now a memory. Outside, the world was a boisterous beast, ready to engulf her in its whirlwind of chaos and thrill. Her body was ablaze with the fevered excitement coursing through her veins, a stark contrast to the cold, indifferent stars scattered across the sky.

The biker gang stood before her, their motorcycles growling like famished predators eager for their next hunt. They exuded an aura tinged with danger, their spirits untamed and unyielding. Amelia's heart skipped a beat as she took in the sight, realizing she was about to become part of this savage pack for the night. The thought both terrified and exhilarated her, a potent cocktail of emotions that set her nerves on edge.

With a devilish grin, Amelia hopped onto the back of a sleek, black motorcycle, gripping tightly onto the leather-clad figure steering the steel beast. The moment she settled into position, their engines roared to life, propelling them forward into the night with a ferocity that defied reason and consequence. The bike vibrated beneath her, a living entity of metal and power, carrying her away from the familiarity of her own despair.

Together, they tore through the desolate streets, igniting a symphony of howls and purrs that reverberated through the starless sky. The wind whipped against Amelia's face, molding her features into a mask of exhilaration and uncertainty. The speed and noise were a form of liberation, a way to drown out the relentless whisper of her inner demons. Amongst the chaos, her eyes fixated on a particular young man, a prospect for the club, who had caught her eye earlier in the evening.

In that fleeting moment, their paths had collided, intertwining their fates like the tendrils of ivy slithering through a cracked brick wall. Amelia sensed a magnetic pull, an inexplicable connection that defied logic but resonated deep within her core. Drawn to the prospect's enigmatic allure, she allowed herself to be swept away into a whirlpool of meth-fueled revelry, surrendering not only her inhibitions but perhaps her very soul. It was a surrender to the unknown, a leap into a void where danger and passion were indistinguishable.

They arrived at the clubhouse, a decrepit building cloaked in shadows and whispers of forgotten debauchery. Inside, the air hung heavy with the acrid scent of chemicals and raucous laughter, an intoxicating mixture that invaded every sense. The walls seemed to breathe with the memories of past excesses, each corner a testament to the lives that had burned brightly and faded away within its confines.

As the night bled into a blurred frenzy of swirling colors and pulsating beats, Amelia and her chosen companion reveled in the twisted pleasures life had allowed them to taste. It was a descent into hedonism, a journey into the depths of human desire and despair. The music throbbed, a relentless pulse that matched the rhythm of her racing heart. Bodies moved in a chaotic dance, a blur of motion and sensation that left her both exhilarated and exhausted.

But little did they know, beneath the surface of their transient euphoria, an unseen darkness loomed, silently observing their every move. The prospect's charm concealed a tormented past stretching far beyond the limits of their tangled existence. His eyes, which had drawn her in with their promise of mystery and excitement, held secrets that were dark and dangerous. In the midst of their newfound infatuation, they were blissfully unaware of the horrors that awaited, lurking in the darkest depths of the night.

The hours passed in a haze of smoke and laughter, each moment blending into the next in a seamless tapestry of excess. Amelia felt herself drawn deeper into the prospect's world, captivated by his charisma and the raw energy that radiated from him. Their connection was intense, a fire that burned brightly against the backdrop of the night's revelry. Yet, beneath the surface, an unspoken tension simmered, a sense of impending doom that neither could shake.

Chapter Forty-Eight

THE AIR WAS ELECTRIC as Amelia stepped into the darkened club, her heart racing in sync with the heavy bass that pounded through the room. This place, so distant from her mundane existence, was a realm where chaos reigned supreme and inhibitions were discarded like forgotten promises. The scent of leather and sweat filled her nostrils, mingling with the pungent aroma of drugs and alcohol, creating an intoxicating atmosphere that ensnared her senses.

Everywhere she turned, bodies were entwined in a primal dance of pleasure, lost in the ecstasy of the moment. Flesh was on unabashed display, desires unleashed without shame. Women with wild, untamed hair indulged in their cravings, their moans of pleasure echoing through the smoke-laden air. Men, their faces contorted in rapture, consumed substances with reckless abandon, driven by a dangerous cocktail of adrenaline and hedonistic desire.

Amelia couldn't help but be mesmerized by the parade of debauchery before her. Her heart thudded erratically, a potent mix of excitement and fear surging through her veins. Her gaze lingered on a group of bikers, their rough exteriors exuding a primal magnetism that drew her closer. They were like mythic creatures, embodiments of a dark allure that promised both danger and exhilaration.

As she approached, she witnessed a man injecting a needle into his arm, his eyes rolling back in a wave of euphoria. Another pair stumbled towards a dimly lit corner, locked in a passionate embrace, lost in a world of their own making. The cacophony of sounds—a symphony of pleasure and pain—enveloped Amelia, threatening to swallow her whole. She was an outsider peering into a world where the rules of society were rendered meaningless.

Out of the chaos emerged the prospect, his eyes gleaming with mischief and adrenaline. He leaned casually against his chopper, beckoning her with a crooked grin that mirrored the mayhem surrounding them. His leather-clad arm extended towards her, offering an escape from the madness. The prospect's presence was magnetic, pulling her towards an abyss of thrilling uncertainty.

Amelia hesitated, a storm of desire and trepidation flooding her mind. Her instincts screamed at her to turn away, to flee from the darkness that whispered seductively in her ear. Yet, something deep within her—a yearning for adventure, a hunger for the unknown—compelled her to take his hand. It was a choice that defied logic, driven by an impulse that she couldn't fully understand.

With a single nod, she surrendered herself to a world that promised to consume her. She climbed onto the back of the roaring machine, feeling its power vibrate beneath her as the prospect revved the engine. The noise drowned out the chaos of the club, creating a bubble of raw energy and anticipation. The bike surged forward, tearing through the night and leaving behind the haze of smoke and lust that lingered at the clubhouse.

As they sped through the desolate streets, the wind whipped through Amelia's hair, carrying her away on a journey she never knew she craved. The city's dark silhouette blurred around her, the line between the living and the dead becoming indistinct. She held on tight, her heart racing in time with the engine's roar. In this moment, she felt a strange liberation, an intoxicating blend of fear and exhilaration that made her feel more alive than ever before.

The world rushed past in a blur, the cityscape giving way to open roads under a starless sky. Amelia's thoughts were a whirlwind, a chaotic jumble of sensations and emotions. The prospect's presence was a steady anchor, his silhouette a dark knight leading her through an adventure that felt both dangerous and irresistibly alluring. Every turn of the road was a new thrill, every acceleration a defiance of the mundane.

Hours seemed to stretch and compress, the passage of time losing all meaning. The thrill of the ride, the closeness of the prospect, and the rush of wind against her face created a perfect storm of sensation. Amelia was no longer just an observer of chaos; she was a participant, a willing accomplice in her own reckless escapade. The darkness that had once whispered to her now roared, a constant companion in her journey.

They finally slowed as the night began to wane, pulling off the road near a secluded spot overlooking the city. The prospect killed the engine, and a profound silence enveloped them, broken only by the distant hum of the city and their own breathing. Amelia dismounted, her legs trembling from the ride and the adrenaline coursing through her.

The prospect lit a cigarette, his face momentarily illuminated by the flame, revealing eyes that held a depth of untold stories. He offered her a smoke, and she took it, inhaling deeply and feeling the burn in her lungs. They stood side by side, two figures on the edge of a precipice, sharing a moment that was both ephemeral and eternal.

In that silence, Amelia felt a strange sense of clarity. The chaos of the club, the thrill of the ride, and the intoxicating presence of the prospect had brought her to this moment of reckoning. She realized that her journey was not just about seeking escape but also about confronting the depths of her own desires and fears. The darkness she had embraced was a part of her, but it did not define her entirely.

As dawn began to break, casting a pale light over the horizon, Amelia knew that her path was still unfolding. The night had been a wild, intoxicating ride, but the new day held the promise of discovery. She was a seeker, an adventurer, navigating the shadows and the light in a world where the boundaries were always shifting. The darkness was a companion, but so was the growing light of dawn, guiding her towards a future that was hers to shape.

Chapter Forty-Nine

IN THE DAWNING LIGHT, they stood locked in a passionate embrace. The air crackled with an intensity that both thrilled and terrified Amelia. Each touch, each kiss, was like stepping into a realm where laws didn't exist and consequences were nothing but distant whispers. The forbidden nature of their tryst added a layer of exhilaration that was impossible to ignore.

As their desires grew bolder, a chill began to creep into the air. The shadows lengthened, twisting and contorting like devious tendrils reaching out to ensnare them. Amelia's mind started to question her impulsive decision, her senses tingling with a sense of unease. What hidden forces lurked in this forsaken place, ready to trap unwary souls?

Despite the doubt clawing at the corners of her mind, she couldn't bring herself to pull away. There was something intoxicating about this forbidden tryst, something that whispered promises of liberation and exhilaration. The prospect's hands roamed her body, guiding her into the realm of the unknown, and she surrendered to the thrill of the moment.

Their passion peaked in a frenzy of raw emotion, but reality soon reared its ugly head. A harsh gust of wind rustled through the air, casting dancing shadows upon the lovers. Amelia's gaze darted around, her heart pounding with a mixture of fear and desire. The whispers of the homeless echoed through the streets, their stories blending with the distant wails of sirens. She and the prospect stood on the precipice of a horror beyond imagination.

Suddenly, the atmosphere shifted. The prospect, who had been her anchor in this chaotic world, changed. Without warning, he reared back and punched Amelia in the face. The impact was immediate and brutal, knocking her out cold. The morning shadows swallowed her whole, plunging her into a darkness that was both literal and metaphorical.

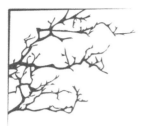

Chapter Fifty

IN THE QUIET DARKNESS of Thornfield, where the streets were deserted and the only sound was the whisper of the wind through the twisted branches of ancient trees, the Boogeyman slumbered fitfully. His bed was a collection of tattered cardboard and threadbare blankets, hidden away in the forgotten recesses of an abandoned building. The nights were long, and each one seemed to stretch into an eternity of cold and isolation. His troubled dreams had become a refuge, a fleeting escape from the oppressive horrors that plagued his existence. But the tranquility he so desperately yearned for was often shattered by the harsh realities of his waking life.

Each day for the Boogeyman was a relentless struggle for survival. The search for food was an arduous and unending quest, fraught with dangers and uncertainty. He would scavenge through garbage bins and abandoned lots, his fingers numb from the cold, his stomach gnawing with hunger. The few scraps he found were rarely enough to stave off the constant ache in his belly. He had long since given up any hope of finding a warm meal or a safe place to rest. His existence was a cruel cycle of desperation and deprivation, a never-ending fight against the elements and his own deteriorating body.

His days were spent in hiding, avoiding the eyes of those who would seek to do him harm. The people of Thornfield had long since labeled him a monster, and their fear and hatred drove them to acts of violence whenever they caught sight of him. He was a pariah, an outcast living on the fringes of society, forever haunted by the darkness that had consumed his life. His only companions were the shadows that clung to him like a second skin, offering a semblance of protection from the harshness of the world.

As night fell, the Boogeyman would retreat to his makeshift shelter, the only place where he felt even the slightest hint of safety. It was here, in the depths of the abandoned building, that he sought the solace of sleep, hoping that his dreams would provide a brief respite from the torment of his waking hours. But even in sleep, he was not free from the horrors that plagued his mind. His dreams were filled with memories of the past, of the violence and pain that had shaped his existence.

On one such night, as the sun began to rise, he lay wrapped in his tattered blankets, the fragile peace of his slumber was shattered by an intrusive sound that wormed its way into his tortured mind—the unmistakable rhythm of fervent intimacy. Curiosity battled against caution within the shadows that sheltered the Boogeyman. He had honed his skills for observation, an art he had mastered through years of silently lurking in the forgotten corners of life. His eyes narrowed, peering like twin orbs of vengeful mystery, fixed upon the source of this deviant symphony.

What he witnessed, however, pierced through the veil of perversion, sending shockwaves of anger pulsating through his very core. The man, consumed by a darkness far deeper than that which the Boogeyman harbored, unleashed a stunning blow upon the defenseless woman. The sickening echo reverberated in the stale air, shaking the very foundation of the voyeur's purpose.

As she lay motionless, a mere pawn to the debased desires of her partner, he continued his vile assault, his actions devoid of remorse and consumed by an insatiable lust. Rage erupted within the Boogeyman, clawing its way to the surface. An indomitable force spurred him forward, surging through the shadows as if propelled by the very anguish that clung to his forsaken soul.

Without hesitation, the Boogeyman launched himself toward the writhing form of the naked man, fueled by righteous fury that had long been suppressed. His fists, once battered and broken, connected with unyielding strength, raining down upon the assailant with an unrelenting vengeance. Blow after blow, fueled by a desire to obscure the lingering darkness that plagued this scene, erupted like a symphony of punishment.

Blood mingled with desperation, despair staining the air as the Boogeyman released his fury upon the wretched man who dared desecrate the innocence of such a fragile vessel. Time lost all meaning as the darkness weaved its web, encompassing the twisted tableau before him. It was a spectacle of retribution, the grotesque dance of justice unfolding beneath a veil of moonlit shadows.

The woman's cries, initially a blend of fear and pain, slowly faded into a stunned silence as she witnessed the Boogeyman's relentless assault. Her eyes, wide with a mixture of terror and disbelief, locked onto the figure that had emerged from the shadows to become her unexpected savior. The Boogeyman's rage was a force of nature, an unyielding tempest that sought to purge the evil before him.

When the man's body finally ceased its struggles, lying motionless and broken beneath the Boogeyman's fists, a heavy silence settled over the scene. The Boogeyman, his breath ragged and his hands bloodied, stared down at the lifeless form with a mixture of satisfaction and revulsion. He had delivered justice, but it had come at a cost—a reminder of the darkness that still resided within him.

He turned to the woman, his expression softening slightly as he saw the fear in her eyes. He extended a hand, a gesture of reassurance, but she recoiled, her body trembling. The Boogeyman understood her reaction; he was a figure of terror, a monster in the eyes of the world. Yet, in this moment, he had been something more—a protector, an avenger.

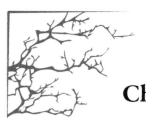

Chapter Fifty-One

AMELIA'S EYES BLINKED open, her vision groggy and disoriented. As the haze lifted, she found herself sprawled on the grimy pavement, the cold touch of damp concrete seeping through her thin jacket. The air around her was thick with the acrid stench of decay and desperation, each breath a reminder of the harsh reality she had woken up to. Confusion swirled within her, like shadows dancing in the dimly lit corner of a forgotten alleyway.

As her senses slowly sharpened, the sight before her unleashed a torrent of terror. A disheveled figure, wild eyes glinting with madness, loomed over a defenseless prospect with a desperate gleam in his hands. The figure was a grotesque amalgamation of human suffering and predatory intent, a living nightmare come to life. A knife, worn and jagged, poised to cut through hope and shred the fragile threads of a future yet unfulfilled.

Instinct flared within Amelia, a primal surge of adrenaline coursing through her veins. The raw, unfiltered need to survive took over, her body reacting faster than her mind could process. With a desperate cry, she sprang to her feet, her body fueled by a determination stronger than her trembling limbs would suggest. Time seemed to slow down, a distorted reality where the ticking of seconds was replaced by the pounding of her own heartbeat.

In that suspended moment, she spotted the prospect's gun, abandoned on the grimy concrete floor, a potential instrument of salvation waiting to be grasped. The cold metal glinted dully in the faint light, a beacon of hope in the suffocating darkness. Without hesitating, she lunged towards it, her fingers wrapping around the cold metal, a steadfast grip that brought a flicker of courage to her soul.

The homeless man turned his gaze towards the sudden movement, eyes now burning with a desperate rage. His face twisted into a mask of fury and desperation, every line etched with a lifetime of hardship and despair. The knife slashed through the air like a beast's fangs, hungering for blood. But Amelia, guided by a force stronger than herself, evaded the deadly edge with a grace that defied her years. Her movements were fluid, almost instinctual, a dance of survival that left no room for error.

The gun trembled in her hands, its weight a paradox of protection and destruction. It was heavy with the potential to save a life but equally capable of ending one. She hesitated for only a split second, but in that fractured sliver of time, she made a choice that would tear apart her reality forever. The gravity of the situation pressed down on her, a crushing force that demanded action despite the fear that gripped her heart.

Fingers white with fear and determination, she squeezed the trigger, unleashing a volley of terror upon the world like a torrential storm. Bang. Bang. Bang. The gun spat flames and hot lead, each shot a testament to the darkness lurking within the human soul. The echoes reverberated through the alley, a symphony of agony and desperation, too loud for the ears of mortals to bear. Each shot was a punctuation mark in the narrative of violence, a brutal assertion of her will to survive.

Nine shots pierced the air, their echoes swallowed by the eternal night. The homeless man's body convulsed, contorted by the force of each bullet's impact, until he crumpled to the ground, a life extinguished in the blink of an eye. The prospect lay gasping for breath, eyes wide with a mix of gratitude and terror. His expression was a mirror of Amelia's own internal conflict, a reflection of the thin line between salvation and damnation.

Trembling, Amelia pocketed the empty gun. Her hands, previously mere extensions of her will, now seemed tainted, forever marked by the sins they had wrought. The weight of her actions settled over her like a suffocating shroud, each breath a struggle against the rising tide of guilt and horror. Pulling out her phone, fingers slick with sweat, she dialed the numbers that held the promise of salvation. The device felt alien in her hands, a lifeline to a world that seemed impossibly distant.

Her voice, in stark contrast to the chaos that unfolded mere moments ago, emerged as a breathless whisper, barely reaching the ears of the unknown responder. The words tumbled out in a disjointed stream, fragments of the nightmare she had just endured. The act of speaking seemed to anchor her to reality, a tenuous connection to a world that was rapidly spinning out of control.

Her words hung heavy in the air, mingling with the scent of gunpowder and the bitter taste of regret. Amelia had changed that night, irrevocably altered by the darkness she had both encountered and brought to life. Each heartbeat echoed with the realization that she had crossed a line, stepped into a realm where morality was blurred and survival demanded a price. Little did she know, however, that the horrors she had experienced were only the beginning of a long, tortuous journey through the depths of her own fears. The path ahead was shrouded in uncertainty, a labyrinth of nightmares that would test the very limits of her endurance.

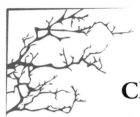

Chapter Fifty-Two

AMELIA'S WORLD, ONCE serene and familiar, shattered into a million jagged pieces as she learned the horrifying truth. The man she had shared an intimate moment with, a prospect desperate for acceptance into the notorious gang, harbored sinister intentions all along. Murder, his twisted path to ascendancy within the blood-soaked ranks of the patch holders, had been his hidden agenda.

But fate, cunning as ever, had woven a different tapestry. In the shadows, a homeless man bore witness to the impending horror. He knew about the gang, their ruthless ways, and what awaited Amelia after she had surrendered to the ecstasy of the night. Driven by an unseen valor, he vowed to save her from the abyss of this demented destiny.

As Amelia stood in the dimly lit alleyway, the weight of her decisions pressing down on her like a suffocating fog, an odd irony pervaded the air. The very Boogeyman who had tormented her in her darkest childhood fears emerged, unexpectedly, as her savior. Memories of Thornfield's haunting halls and its malevolent occupant flooded back, evoking a confusing cocktail of terror and gratitude.

Amelia's childhood had been marred by nightmares of the Boogeyman, a faceless terror lurking in the shadows, waiting to claim her. Those nights, filled with heart-pounding fear and sleepless hours, had left an indelible mark on her psyche. Yet now, in a twisted turn of fate, that same figure had stepped out of the recesses of her mind to offer her salvation.

The homeless man, cloaked in the rags of destitution and the weight of his own haunted past, had followed the gang's movements for years. He knew their every hideout, their every cruel initiation rite. When he saw Amelia with the prospect, his heart had clenched with a resolve he hadn't felt in decades. This young woman, oblivious to the peril she was in, reminded him of someone he had lost long ago. His mission to save her became not just a rescue, but a redemption.

Thus, as life twisted its fragile threads into a bewildering tapestry, fate played its final hand. In the pulse-pounding chaos that ensued, Amelia, in a moment of unforgiving panic, unleashed a burst of gunfire. A bullet flew with menacing precision, finding its home in the heart of the Boogeyman who had become her salvation. The homeless man, who had cast aside his own fears to protect her, crumpled to the ground, his life extinguished in a cruel twist of destiny.

As the echoes of gunfire faded into the night, Amelia stood frozen, the reality of her actions crashing down upon her. Her hands, stained with the blood of her unintended victim, shook violently. The sunrise, once a beautiful backdrop to her nightly escapades, now seemed like a stage where the tragic play of her life had unfolded. Her breath came in short, ragged gasps as she tried to process what had just happened.

Awash in a potent blend of relief and despair, Amelia mourned the passing of her unlikely savior. The Boogeyman, now forever silenced, had ultimately met his deserved demise. The streets, once ruled by his terror, breathed a collective sigh of freedom, the chains of their torment loosening. Yet, the irony of it all gnawed at her soul—her savior had fallen by her own hand, a grim reminder of the darkness that lurked within her.

Tears streamed down Amelia's face as she looked at the lifeless body before her. "I'm sorry," she whispered, her voice trembling with emotion. The weight of guilt pressed heavily on her chest, making it hard to breathe. She felt as if the walls of the alley were closing in on her, suffocating her with the enormity of what she had done.

Amelia's journey, though fraught with peril and haunted by unspeakable horrors, carried her to an unexpected destination—a place of liberation, tinged with the lingering shadows of remorse. She walked away from the scene, each step heavy with the burden of her actions, her mind replaying the nightmarish sequence of events that had led her to this point.

The Boogeyman's reign of terror, perpetuated by fate's twisted games, had finally come to an end. The stories of his cruelty would fade into the annals of the city's dark history, replaced by tales of his unexpected act of heroism. Yet, as Amelia stood amidst the wreckage of her ordeal, she couldn't help but wonder if her salvation had truly cost her soul, forever damned in the relentless grip of guilt.

Amelia knew that her journey was far from over. The path ahead was uncertain, fraught with the ghosts of her past and the shadows of her guilt. Yet, in the depths of her despair, a glimmer of hope remained. Perhaps, in time, she could find a way to reconcile her actions and find peace. Until then, she would carry the memory of the Boogeyman—the unlikely savior who had given his life for hers—as a beacon of both warning and hope.

As she walked away from the scene, the morning seemed colder, the dawn more oppressive. Amelia wrapped her arms around herself, seeking comfort in the face of overwhelming despair. She had been given a second chance, but at what cost? The Boogeyman's sacrifice weighed heavily on her heart, a constant reminder of the fragility of life and the thin line between good and evil.

Each step forward felt like a struggle, her legs heavy with the weight of her sorrow. She had taken a life, and that knowledge would haunt her forever. But as she looked up at the morning sky, she saw a single star shining brightly. It was a small reminder that even in the darkest times, there could be a glimmer of light. And with that thought, Amelia resolved to honor the Boogeyman's memory by seeking a path of redemption, one step at a time.

Chapter Fifty-Three

AMELIA HAD ALWAYS BEEN haunted. The shadows of her past clung to her like a relentless fog, an ever-present reminder of the horrors that had once consumed her. She had fought and vanquished her own personal Boogeyman, the demon that had lurked in her mind, threatening to tear her apart from within. But in doing so, she had inadvertently killed her savior, that last fragment of hope that had kept her going.

The weight of her heavy heart grew unbearable, like an anchor dragging her down into the depths of despair. She felt the crushing grip of helplessness tightening around her neck, and a thought began to crystallize in her mind – the notion that perhaps if she were to end it all, the torment would finally cease. Amelia had always been a fighter, but even the strongest warriors eventually grow weary.

Each day became a relentless struggle, a ceaseless battle against the overwhelming tide of her own anguish. Nights offered no respite; they were haunted by the echoes of her past, the gunfire that had sealed her fate reverberating in her mind. She was caught in a never-ending loop of torment, each moment more unbearable than the last. The guilt of her actions weighed heavily upon her soul, an unshakable burden she could not escape.

One fateful night, she stood on that bridge, a place where hopes and dreams meet the cruel edge of reality. The river flowed beneath, a reflection of her own turbulent emotions, and as she approached the precipice of her existence, a morbid curiosity urged her to peer into the abyss below. The swirling darkness seemed almost inviting, offering a whispered seduction of release. The city's lights flickered in the distance, indifferent to her plight, as if mocking her pain.

Unyielding determination guided her trembling hands as she fashioned a makeshift noose, a symbol of her surrender to the overwhelming darkness that had plagued her very soul. The rope constricted around her neck, a physical manifestation of the suffocating pain suffusing her every breath. The rough fibers bit into her skin, each strand a testament to her despair. With one last wavering glance skyward, she took that final step into the unknown.

Time seemed to stand still as gravity seized hold of her fragile form, dragging her mercilessly towards her perceived salvation. For a fleeting moment, she felt the icy tendrils of freedom intertwining with her very being, as if her troubles were being washed away in the rush of the wind. The cold air whipped around her, a stark contrast to the burning agony within. But fate had other plans.

Amelia hung there, a macabre spectacle dancing upon the precipice between life and death. The rope, as if reluctant to fulfill its intended purpose, refused to snap that tenuous connection. Inexplicably, she gasped for breath, her body wracked with pain and terror. It was not a quick descent into oblivion, nor a merciful exit from the labyrinth of her own anguish. Her mind screamed for release, but her body clung stubbornly to life.

As her body swung like a pendulum, she felt the searing sting of the rope against her throat, her vocal cords ravaged by the unforgiving embrace. The realization hit her like a thunderclap – she would never speak again. The very essence of her essence, stolen by the forsaken act that had failed to grant her release. The pain was excruciating, each breath a battle for survival. The loss of her voice was not just a physical injury but a profound symbol of her silenced cries for help, her inability to communicate her suffering.

In the midst of her torment, the world around her blurred into a haze of pain and despair. Her vision darkened at the edges, her senses dulled by the relentless onslaught of agony. She was barely aware of her surroundings, her mind consumed by the overwhelming desire for an end that had eluded her. The realization that she had failed in her final act of desperation was a cruel twist of fate, a reminder of the inescapable torment that had driven her to this point.

As her body swayed, the physical pain merged with the emotional agony that had plagued her for so long. The memories of her past, the guilt of her actions, and the weight of her unfulfilled life all converged in a maelstrom of suffering. She was trapped in a cycle of torment, unable to escape the horrors that had defined her existence.

Amelia's mind began to drift, her thoughts scattered and disjointed. She thought of the moments that had led her here, the choices she had made, and the paths she had taken. Each memory was a jagged shard, cutting through her consciousness with relentless precision. She had sought solace in death, but found only more pain, a cruel irony that gnawed at her soul.

As the minutes stretched into an eternity, Amelia's strength waned. Her body grew weaker, her grip on life slipping away. The pain became a dull throb, the edges of her consciousness fraying as she hovered on the brink of oblivion. In those final moments, she felt a profound sense of resignation, a reluctant acceptance of her fate. She had fought so hard, but in the end, it seemed that her struggles had been in vain.

Yet, even in the depths of her despair, a small spark of determination remained. It was a fragile flicker, a remnant of the strength that had carried her through so many trials. It was the part of her that refused to give up, that clung to the hope of redemption, no matter how distant it seemed. It was this spark that kept her hanging on, that refused to let her surrender completely to the darkness.

And so, Amelia hung there, suspended between life and death, her body a testament to the battle raging within her soul. She had sought an end, but found only more pain. She had tried to escape, but found herself trapped in a new kind of torment.

Perhaps this was the only way by which her never-ending pain would be put to rest. She had been a fighter all her life. From childhood to youth, all she had been doing was fighting her demons. She was exhausted and tired. The relentless battles had drained her of her strength, leaving her a mere shell of the person she once was. She could not see the glimmer of hope anymore, and ending it all might give her the peace she had been seeking in her living life. The constant struggle, the ceaseless war against her inner torment, had worn her down to the point where she could no longer bear the weight of her own existence.

This is how it ends, perhaps. This is how it would've ended up for her. For fighting for so many years and now giving up, was the fight worth it? Maybe yes. She had fought valiantly, with every ounce of strength she could muster, but the battles had taken their toll. The fighter in Amelia was losing its breath with every second passing. Each moment felt like an eternity, her spirit weakening as the pain became unbearable. The fight had been long and arduous, and now, standing at the precipice of her existence, she questioned whether it had all been in vain. But the fatigue was overwhelming, and the will to continue slipping away like sand through her fingers.

Chapter Fifty-Four

SITTING IN HER COLD, sterile room at the sanitarium, Amelia realized that her worst fears had been realized. The Boogeyman was real. A creature that defied logic and the nature of life itself. No matter how desperately one tried to kill him, he would always return, like a relentless specter of darkness, a perpetual shadow that clung to her every thought and dream.

It had begun innocently enough. Shadows lurking in the corners of her vision. An unexplained breeze whispering through her room, carrying with it a tinge of malevolence that sent chills down her spine. But as the sightings intensified, Amelia's world crumbled around her, piece by horrifying piece. The rational explanations she clung to were shattered, replaced by an ever-growing terror that gnawed at her sanity.

The first time she saw him, really saw him, was in the reflection of her bathroom mirror. The room had been silent, the kind of silence that presses against your eardrums and makes your skin crawl. She had been brushing her teeth when she noticed the dark figure standing just behind her. His eyes, two pits of endless night, bore into her soul. She had spun around, but the room was empty. Yet, the feeling of being watched, of being hunted, remained.

Now, locked away from the outside world, Amelia sought solace in a room devoid of shadows. The walls were painted a stark white, the lights always on, day and night, ensuring that not even a sliver of darkness could penetrate her fortress of security. But despite these precautions, she trembled uncontrollably, fear coursing through her veins like icy tendrils. The constant illumination did little to quell the dread that had taken root in her heart.

The nurses, with their kind faces and gentle hands, couldn't understand. They saw a frightened woman, but they couldn't comprehend the depth of her terror. They didn't see the Boogeyman, didn't feel his oppressive presence. They assured her that it was all in her head, that she was safe. But Amelia knew better. The Boogeyman was real, and he was coming for her.

Sleep became a rare commodity for Amelia, a luxury she could ill afford. Only when her body succumbed to the point of complete exhaustion would her mind slip into merciful unconsciousness. And even then, the dreams that plagued her were filled with the haunting presence of the Boogeyman, lurking in the recesses of her nightmares, waiting for the perfect moment to strike. She would wake up screaming, drenched in sweat, her heart pounding as if it would burst from her chest.

In these dreams, she was a child again, hiding under her bed, the covers pulled tight around her. She could hear the Boogeyman's ragged breathing, feel his cold breath on her skin. He whispered to her, promises of pain and suffering that chilled her to the bone. She would wake up just as his clawed hand reached for her, the image seared into her mind.

Amelia had become a permanent resident of her own personal hell, held captive by the very monster she once believed to be a myth. The sanitarium, which was meant to be a place of healing, had become her prison. She yearned for the release of death, but knew that even in death, the Boogeyman would find her. He was an entity that transcended the physical realm, a force of darkness that could not be extinguished. The knowledge of his persistence was a weight that crushed her spirit.

Days blended into nights, an endless cycle of fear and exhaustion. Her body grew frail, her once bright eyes dull and haunted. She barely ate, food tasting like ash in her mouth. The doctors spoke in hushed tones, their pitying glances a constant reminder of her plight. They increased her medication, hoping to numb her fear, but nothing could touch the deep-seated terror that had taken hold of her.

So she clung to her fragile existence, tiptoeing on the edge of madness, forever haunted by the Boogeyman. She warned anyone who would listen, her voice a thin, reedy whisper. "Beware," she would say, her eyes wide with fear. "Beware the Boogeyman, for he will find you. One way or another, you will succumb to his insidious grasp and once you do, there is no escape." Her words were met with nods of understanding, but she could see the disbelief in their eyes. They thought her mad, a victim of her own mind.

But Amelia knew the truth. She knew that the Boogeyman was real, that he was out there, waiting. Every creak of the floor, every rustle of the leaves outside her window, sent her heart racing. She was a prisoner of her fear, and there was no escape.

They say the last thing she ever said, before her vocal cords finally quit working altogether, was a haunting testament to her despair. As the blaring of horns echoed through the sky, a cacophony that seemed to herald the end of her sanity, she dropped to her knees and whispered, "I'll see you on the dark side of the moon." Her voice, barely audible, carried a weight of sorrow and resignation that sent shivers down the spines of those who heard it.

The staff found her there, kneeling on the cold, sterile floor, her eyes vacant and her spirit broken. Her words echoed in their minds, a chilling reminder of the darkness that lurked within the human soul. They gently lifted her, their touch gentle yet firm, guiding her back to her bed. They spoke soothing words, but Amelia no longer heard them. She was lost in her own world, a place where shadows danced and the Boogeyman reigned supreme.

Amelia's story became a cautionary tale, whispered among the patients and staff of the sanitarium. Her descent into madness, her battle against an unseen terror, was a stark reminder of the fragile line between reality and the horrors of the mind. Her final words, cryptic and foreboding, lingered in the air, a haunting epitaph to a life consumed by fear.

In the end, Amelia's fight was not in vain. Her warnings, though dismissed by many, found their way into the hearts of those who listened. The Boogeyman, whether a figment of her imagination or a real entity, served as a symbol of the darkness that can consume us all. Amelia's struggle, her bravery in the face of insurmountable fear, became a beacon for those who battled their own demons.

And so, Amelia remained a ghostly figure in the annals of the sanitarium's history. Her room, once a place of terror, was left untouched, a silent memorial to her fight. The lights, always on, cast a perpetual glow, warding off the shadows that had once tormented her. And in the stillness, one could almost hear her whisper, a final warning from beyond the grave.

"Beware the Boogeyman, for he will find you. One way or another, you will succumb to his insidious grasp. And once you do, there is no escape."

With her last breath, Amelia had become a part of the legend, her story a chilling reminder of the darkness that lurks within us all. The Boogeyman, whether real or imagined, continued to haunt the corners of the mind, a testament to the power of fear and the indomitable human spirit that fights against it.

Epilogue:
"The Red Pill"

In the twisted realm of Thornfield, a place where the sun seemed perpetually eclipsed and shadows danced with malicious intent, darkness and despair clung to the very air like a suffocating shroud. The trees, gnarled and twisted, reached out like skeletal fingers, their branches creaking under the weight of countless whispered fears. The cobblestone streets, slick with an unending rain, reflected the dim light of flickering lanterns, casting an eerie glow that seemed to bleed into the very fabric of the town. It was a place where hope was a distant memory, where the cries of the desperate and the damned formed a constant, mournful dirge.

In this forsaken corner of the world, there lived a man who was both feared and despised. Known as The Boogeyman, his name was whispered through the hushed, trembling voices of those who dared to speak of him. He was the embodiment of evil, haunting the nightmares of the innocent with an omnipresence that defied understanding. His presence was a lingering dread, a palpable force that seeped into the bones of Thornfield's inhabitants, leaving them cold and fearful. The Boogeyman was not merely a figure of folklore or ghost stories; he was a living nightmare, a dark legend whose malevolent influence seemed to stretch beyond the physical world and into the very souls of those who dwelled in his shadow.

Now, in a place beyond earthly comprehension, he stood before God Himself. The divine light bathed his scarred and hollowed features, casting an eerie glow upon his ashen skin. God, with eyes as deep and endless as the cosmos, looked upon him with unwavering scrutiny.

"What say you of your time upon the earthly realm?" God's voice rumbled, a thunderous and somber symphony that sent tremors through the very essence of the Boogeyman's being.

The man's lips trembled, though no words were uttered. The heavy weight of futility hung around him like chains, a mute testimony to the cruelty of his existence. He gazed into the all-knowing eyes of God, seeking solace in a realm where such redemption seemed an impossibility.

"They offered me no hope," the man's thoughts whispered within the confines of his tortured mind. "In a world where darkness held sway, I was a forgotten casualty; a silent voice drowned amidst the clamor of the uncaring masses."

In life, he was naught but a wretched figure, a mute unable to defend himself, a lost soul condemned to wander the desolate streets. Arrested time and time again for crimes of desperation, he found himself trapped within a cycle of suffering. The world branded him a vagrant, a thief, and a predator. A label he could not escape, as it seeped into his very pores and stained his soul.

An incident unfolded, forever marking the pages of his torment. A simple act of nature's call, exposed to the critical eye of a young boy and his fuming mother. The police, summoned by this perceived transgression, became tormentors, raining merciless blows upon him both physically and emotionally.

Charges were filed, igniting the flames of indignity. Branded a registered sex offender, a label that poisoned every interaction, he retreated into the cold embrace of an abandoned house. Within its decaying walls, he found solace in the hidden rooms and forgotten crawlspaces.

But even in this sanctuary, irony leered at him with cruel laughter. A family, unknowing of his presence, moved into his refuge. And it was the daughter, a child who had become a jagged shard of innocence, who whispered that haunting name in fear and trembling – Boogeyman.

Arrested once more, the Boogeyman was condemned to a new depth of despair. The police, their patience unraveling thread by thread, piled more charges onto his broken shoulders, falsifying testimony and reports as well as planting evidence. They longed to rid themselves of this specter, this abomination that clawed at their collective sanity.

Prison became his new abode, a purgatory of torment and suffering. But release was his bitter companion once more, thrusting him back into a world that hunted him, thirsty for vengeance. Beaten, violated, and set ablaze, he clung to existence with unyielding desperation.

Years slipped away, cloaked in the silent agony of a coma. And yet, his return to the waking world offered no respite from the dark clutches of persecution. Hunted once again, like a twisted game of prey and predator, he bore witness to the depths of human cruelty and the terrifying silence of indifference.

God's heavy sigh resounded like a requiem, a lamentation for a soul lost in the stormy sea of humanity's damning flaws. His gaze, heavy with sorrow and an unspoken regret, fell upon the Boogeyman.

"Gabriel," God's voice commanded, carrying a melancholic weight. "Blow your horn, for this is a tale severed from salvation."

So, as the cry of Gabriel's horn resonated through the heavens, the Boogeyman's existence dissolved into melancholic whispers, swallowed by the all-encompassing abyss of eternity. A tragedy untethered, lost in the realms where hope and redemption could never truly find purchase.

The sound cut through the air like a razor through flesh, slicing through the mundane routines and banalities of everyday life. It was a sound that transcended distance, time, and even death itself. It was the unmistakable blow of Gabriel's horn, heralding the final act in the macabre play of existence.

No one could escape its grasp, for it seeped into every crevice, every corner of the world. It infiltrated the bustling cities with their concrete jungles, causing even the most jaded hearts to skip a beat. It invaded the serene countryside, echoing through the rolling hills and whispering secrets to the deaf ears of the trees. It resonated through the desolate wastelands, an eerie symphony that stirred the dust and awakened the souls of the long-departed.

Men and women, young and old, found themselves frozen in their tracks, gripped by a primal fear that crawled up their spines like a legion of spiders. The weight of their sins bore down on them like a crushing burden, as they realized the futility of their existence. It was a relentless reminder of their mortality, of the fragility of life's illusions.

As the horn blew, the earth quivered beneath their trembling feet. The ground cracked and fissured, revealing the chilling abyss that lay dormant below. With each resounding note, the dead clawed their way out of their eternal slumber, rising from the soil with grotesque determination. The once tranquil cemeteries became battlegrounds of the past and present, where the living and the dead converged in a horrifying dance of doom.

Millions fell to their knees, their voices choked with desperation, uttering fervent prayers and pleas for salvation. They reached out towards the heavens, as if hoping to find solace in a benevolent deity. Yet, there was no respite to be found, for there are no second chances when faced with the impending final act.

The symphony of chaos engulfed the world, as humanity grappled with the harsh reality of their inevitable demise. Families clung to one another, their tear-streaked faces a tapestry of despair and regret. Governments crumbled under the weight of their powerlessness, their promises of security exposed as hollow lies. Faith was tested, shattered, and discarded like broken shards of glass.

In those final moments, the flaws and failures of mankind were laid bare for all to see. The deafening sound of Gabriel's horn stripped away the masks of our superficial existence, revealing the rawness and vulnerability that lurked beneath. It was a reckoning, a sobering reminder of our shared mortality and the indelible marks we leave upon the world.

As the last note faded into eternity, a silence descended upon the ravaged earth. The human race, poised on the precipice of oblivion, was left with nothing but echoes of regrets and unspoken words. The world, once teeming with life and possibility, became a desolate wasteland, a haunting testament to what once was.

In the end, all that was left was the haunting melody of Gabriel's horn, resonating through the eternities. It was a melancholic requiem, a reminder that existence is but a fleeting dance of light amidst the darkness. And as the echoes of that mournful sound reverberated through the annals of time, the earth succumbed to its final slumber, an eternal silence blanketing the remnants of humanity's hubris and despair.

Thus, the story of the Boogeyman and the world he tormented came to its sorrowful conclusion, a poignant tale of redemption denied, and the relentless pursuit of peace that remained ever elusive. As the cosmos continued its silent march, the Boogeyman's legacy lingered, a dark shadow cast over the memories of those who had dared to believe in hope, only to be swallowed by the abyss of eternal night.

"Be not forgetful to entertain strangers: for thereby some have entertained angels unawares." – *Hebrews 13:2*

Did you love *Boogeyman*? Then you should read *The Madcap Adventures of Max and Lilly*[1] by Andrew C. Howard!

[2]

Lilly and Max had a dream for this summer vacation. A dream to stream. But the plan to binge the hot days away falls apart when they are sucked into a cursed TV and transported to an interstellar tv network where they are told they will have to survive a gauntlet of shows that turn out to be more real than they ever imagined. Now, they have to live the shows they wanted to watch, and each episode is life or death.

Behind it all, an evil presence pulls the strings. A mysterious magical mastermind, obsessed with this ultimate streaming universe and a misplaced vendetta against the teens. Between that and a hostile takeover of the space station, he literally runs the show. But where he

---

1. https://books2read.com/u/mlG22q

2. https://books2read.com/u/mlG22q

came from and what he wants is as unknown as what he did to the previous producer, or what he plans to do next with Max and Lilly.

It's time to find out if these armchair critics can really do a better job than the characters in the shows they love. And if they succeed, if they survive, what will the wizard do then?

Also by Andrew C. Howard

Boogeyman
The Madcap Adventures of Max and Lilly

About the Author

Andrew is the only son of Sarah and Kenneth Howard. He graduated from St. Phillips College in 2016. Andrew is a musician who performs under the name "Blue" and is also an actor. This is his second novel, with the first being *The Madcap Adventures of Max and Lilly*.

Milton Keynes UK
Ingram Content Group UK Ltd.
UKHW042240011124
450424UK00001BA/123